About *The Delivery*

Wilbur is an unassuming little man living an unassuming little life. He and his wife have a stereotypical 1950s existence, but in modern America.

One day, he arrives home to discover a mysterious crate. His attempts to deal with a seemingly minor mistake lead to an escalating series of absurdities, straining his marriage, leaving the couple's lives in tatters, and leading him to question his place in the world.

Do millions perish? Does the world end? Does Wilbur figure out how to make photocopies? The Delivery is what happens when Kafka meets Monty Python.

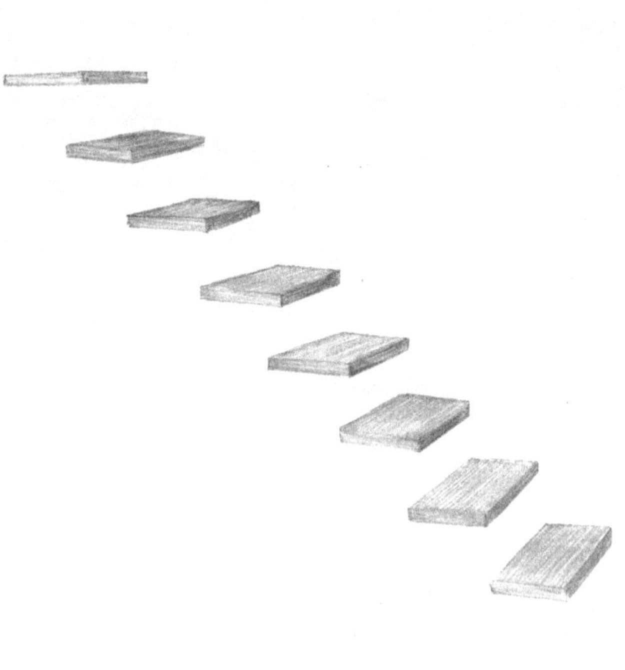

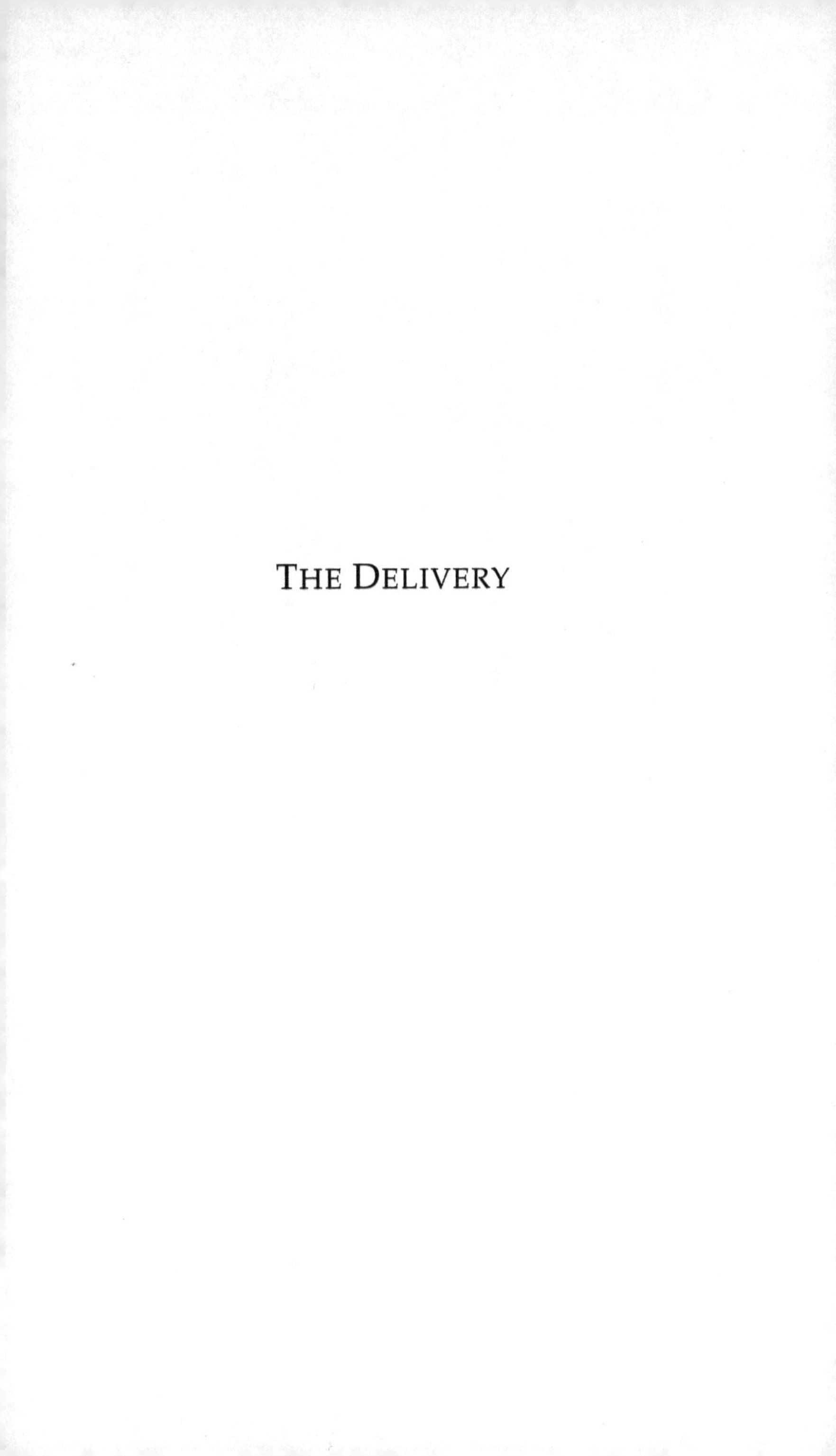

THE DELIVERY

THE DELIVERY

by

K.M. Halpern

Ɛpsilon Books

ISBN-13 (paperback): 978-1-945671-11-1

ISBN-13 (ebook): 978-1-945671-12-8

Library of Congress Control Number: 2021902595

Published by Epsilon Books

Printed in the United States of America

Cover Art by Sara Zieve Miller

First Edition

CONTENTS

Chapter 1   1

Chapter 2   27

Chapter 3   45

Chapter 4   61

Chapter 5   69

Chapter 6   79

Chapter 7   107

Chapter 8   125

Chapter 9   137

Chapter 10   155

Chapter 1

The nice thing about coming home was that anything could be waiting. The nicer thing was that nothing ever was.

Wilbur was about to hang his hat on the hall rack, when a shrill voice issued from the house.

"You got a package."

It felt pointless to announce himself now, so he just mumbled "I'm home, hon." Then he recomposed his face, a twice-daily ritual.

"What is it, hon?" he called out.

There was no reply.

He took two steps toward the living room but felt heavy. Patting himself up and down, Wilbur realized he hadn't finished. He removed his coat and deposited the contents of his pockets into a small tray by the door. It seemed unsafe to place his wallet in plain sight of the glass-panel door. Of course, there was nothing to fear in this neighborhood. It was a safe neighborhood. But that didn't mean he should tempt people. What was the old saying? A lock was to keep sane people sane. Or was it to keep honest people sane? Glass panels probably wouldn't keep people sane or honest, but they were what Sarah wanted.

Disburdened, Wilbur took a deep breath and entered the living room.

"I'm home, hon," he called out absentmindedly.

"I kind of figured that out," came a muffled reply,

though Wilbur couldn't tell from where. It was an uncanny ability of his wife, this lack of directionality. It certainly wasn't lack of direction. She never could be accused of that. However rudderless he felt at times, she always knew exactly what she wanted and how. He envied this when he wasn't cursing it.

"What is it?" Wilbur asked.

"What is what?" It was a normal voice, an embodied voice. Bedroom. She was in the bedroom, and Wilbur knew what *that* meant. He sighed and plopped down on the couch. There was no telling how long she would be vacuuming up there. The bedroom had been an unholy mess in the morning.

In fact, this had troubled him all day at work, a flea in the back of his mind. Not that the bedroom was a mess, but that it still was a mess on a Wednesday. Sarah always vacuumed on Tuesdays and never this late in the day. She must have been busy with other things. Or was it an excuse to be busy while he was home?

"When's dinner, hon?" he called out.

There was a pause before Sarah replied. Wilbur couldn't tell what was behind that pause, and he decided he didn't care. He had been deciding that a lot lately. At forty-six, he just didn't have the energy to care. Then he remembered the package.

He glanced at the credenza, where the mail usually awaited. A few bills were carefully laid out. Darn it, Sarah must have discarded the junk mail. Wilbur preferred to do this himself. What if they won the sweepstakes, and she accidentally threw away the prize money?

Wilbur once again scanned the credenza. No

package. The credenza was where mail went. Packages too, unless they were large.

Maybe the package was large, and she'd put it on the floor. He looked around but saw nothing.

"Where's the package?"

No reply.

"Hon?"

A faint "yeah?"

"Where's the package, hon?"

"Oh, that." His wife's easy tone allayed any worry. There wasn't an argument brewing, some silent resentment to find voice at the least opportune time. She just was distracted with cleaning.

"Yeah?" he called out when nothing followed. The vacuum cleaner hummed overhead. Maybe she couldn't hear him. He was about to go upstairs, when she replied.

"In the basement."

Why would Sarah put it in the basement? She never went into the basement. Wilbur considered asking but could think of no neutral way to frame the question. It would seem a criticism, or be one. He wasn't sure it shouldn't be. What sort of person put packages in the basement? The credenza was where mail went. Packages too, unless they were large.

"Thanks," he yelled.

The only reply was the wheezing vacuum. It seemed to be asking for something, a gasping plea for respite, to be removed from the world. Until next time. Or maybe it just was asthmatic. That would make sense given what it had to breathe.

Wilbur sometimes felt like he understood

machines better than people these days, or maybe the people just seemed more like machines.

~•~

Wilbur's toe hurt. Not enough to merit profanity, just regret. At least he hadn't fallen down the stairs. With the light off, that easily could have happened. The concern wasn't new, but the stubbed toe was.

He should have installed a switch at the top of the stairs or at least left the door ajar. Wilbur resolved to be more careful in the future but knew he wouldn't, for the same reason he only buckled up once his car was moving. It didn't make sense, but it didn't have to. It just was.

His hand searched for a few seconds until it located a dangling chain. The dark wasn't dispelled, just diminished. Wilbur doubted the dark truly could be dispelled. It was absence, and absence always won in the end.

The lighting in the basement was weak. This was another thing Wilbur easily could have attended to, but he felt it was a waste of money. Besides, he wasn't sure he wanted to see things clearly. Seeing things clearly was overrated. The world was less interesting precise. Indistinct shapes were pregnant with mystery, beings of true potential. Once he knew what was in a box, it gained definition, became stuff. Whatever that stuff was, it just was stuff. Plain old stuff.

His eyes slowly adjusted to the dim light. That was the other reason Wilbur didn't upgrade the bulbs. The faint illumination made him feel catlike, lethal. Maybe it was better for his eyes, would train them. Maybe he would become catlike, lethal. Or trip and break his neck. Either way, it would be a change.

A throbbing in his toe reminded him that not all change was good. The cause of that pain soon became clear. The large open space at the bottom of the stairs had something in it. Something large. Wilbur groaned the moment he saw it.

There could be no mistaking the room's new occupant. The basement was not fancy, or even finished. The floor was concrete, and the ceiling uncovered. It was full height, thank goodness. Wilbur hated dropped cellar ceilings. He wasn't a tall man, but he wasn't short either. With all the wires and bulbs and pipes, anything but a full height ceiling was a chore to work under. Not that any work happened under this ceiling.

The room itself was a thirty foot by twenty foot rectangle narrowed by worktables along the two sides, the staircase at one end, and various heating equipment at the other. What space there was, Wilbur did his best to keep clear. The basement wasn't spacious, but neither was it cramped. Most important, it was his. It often seemed like the only thing which was. He viewed the intruder with more irritation than curiosity.

Wilbur hadn't ordered anything, and certainly not anything this big. He had a hard time imagining what he *could* order that was so large. For the briefest moment, he suspected it was a surprise from Sarah. The absurdity of the thought almost made him laugh. When had his wife ever been inclined to surprise him with a gift?

It had to be a mistake. Of course it was. What else could it be? That meant it belonged to somebody else and had to be returned. Wilbur did not relish the prospect of arranging a pickup, managing paperwork, and dealing with workers. He envisioned the deliverymen damaging, or even stealing, the things he kept down there as they retrieved their silly crate. He'd probably end up footing the shipping bill too. Somehow, he'd get blamed and have to pay. Not to mention the earful he would get from Sarah. No doubt she would hold him responsible for the whole fiasco. After all, it was in his basement.

Wilbur wondered how quickly he'd be able to get rid of the thing. First he needed to know what he was dealing with, and that meant a closer look. The box ran almost the entire length of the open space, spanned a third of its width, and was as tall as wide. It wasn't made of cheap pine, as Wilbur first supposed. Even without opening the crate, he could tell the wood was solid and heavy.

The latches weren't typical flimsy affairs either. They were solid steel. Twelve heavy padlocks graced the long top edges, six on each side. They seemed like overkill, but Wilbur found them strangely comforting. Faced with such formidable obstacles, he wouldn't be tempted to open the thing. Then he noticed the keys, also hefty. What use were padlocks with keys in them? Well, it *was* meant to be a delivery. It made sense they would provide keys. But why not supply them in a separate bag?

Wilbur wondered whom the crate actually belonged to. It looked expensive. Very expensive.

His eyes lingered on the nearest key. He turned away, ashamed to have considered such a thing, then hurried to the stairs and reached for the light cord.

His hand stopped. How had they gotten the crate into the basement? It was too large to fit through the doorway, let alone make it down the stairs. Had they disassembled it? That seemed farfetched. Why would they reassemble it afterward? This was a delivery. The crate's destination. The crate's destiny.

Wilbur found his wife in the kitchen fussing over something or other. He never understood how she organized the kitchen or what all her something-or-others were. It was her space, much as the basement was his.

"Did you find the package?" Sarah asked while wrangling something in the sink.

Was there a hint of laughter in her voice? It was hard to tell through the noise. A prank seemed unlike her, but that would make it all the more effective.

"You could say that," he replied. His deliberate ambiguity drew no response.

Wilbur's theory quickly lost its luster. If it was a joke, how did Sarah get the crate into the basement? He couldn't even imagine seasoned movers accomplishing such a thing. Maybe the joke was that something so preposterous had been sent to him, but this too made no sense. Sarah wasn't likely to greet such a thing with humor or even indifference. Once again, the predicament arose: how to broach the subject without appearing plaintive.

He placed his arms around Sarah and leaned in to kiss her. She turned toward him but returned only a perfunctory peck on his cheek.

Her eyes drifted to his chest and suddenly grew puzzled, then sharp — as if seeing him for the first time.

"A blue tie."

He hadn't noticed. And apparently neither had she that morning. No, that wasn't it. She'd received a phone call while he was getting ready and hadn't seen him off. He wondered about that phone call. She never got phone calls. Not in the morning.

"Why are you wearing a blue tie?" Sarah asked. There was no reproach in her tone, just confusion. "You always wear a red tie," she continued slowly, as if speaking to herself. "Who wears a blue tie to work?"

A wave of shame rolled over Wilbur. What sort of person, indeed. He hoped she wouldn't ask why he even owned a blue tie, and suddenly realized he did not know. Had someone given it to him? He couldn't think of anyone who gave him ties. Wasn't that what children did? He just had reached into the drawer as usual, and this was what came out. Maybe other things were hiding there, things which one day would emerge to impeach him.

"I just don't understand why you would do such a thing," Sarah reiterated. Her voice had grown sad, doubtful.

Wilbur felt an overwhelming need to justify

himself. "I didn't even know it was there," he swore.

Sarah seemed not to hear him, steadily looking through her husband. She muttered something before turning to face the sink.

"I'm sorry," Wilbur offered, unsure what else to say. Then he realized that the offending article still was attached to him. Rid of it, perhaps he could be redeemed.

He gave the tie a hasty tug, almost choking himself. Disengaging it with greater care, he tossed it in the garbage can. Sarah glanced at the trash but said nothing.

"It was odd there was no label," Wilbur observed, gently rubbing the cheek she'd kissed.

"On the tie?" Sarah asked.

"On the delivery."

"There wasn't?" she replied in a distracted tone.

Maybe it *was* a joke. It was hard to tell from behind. The subtle shaking of her body could be quiet laughter or sobbing or the scrubbing of pots.

"How did you know it was for me?" he asked.

The sink noise stopped, and Sarah turned with a bewildered expression. "Who else would it be for?"

He shrugged and gestured at her.

"I didn't order anything."

"Neither did I," he noted.

"Well, *was* it for me?" she asked.

"I'm not sure."

Sarah raised an eyebrow.

"I didn't open it," he explained.

"That's your choice," she allowed without lowering her eyebrow. Wilbur wondered whether it would start to hurt if held that way for too long. Maybe it would get stuck. Would she be more or less attractive with a permanently furrowed eyebrow?

His eyes lowered to meet hers. "Is it really for me?" He had meant to ask whether it was a joke, but somehow this was all he could muster.

Sarah grabbed a nearby hand-towel and gave her hands an impatient wipe.

"What's this about, Wilbur? Out with it." She never called him by name except when annoyed. Not angry, just annoyed. When he was too hesitant or wishy-washy about something. Yet there was no irritation in her voice, just a certain directness. Did she think he wanted something from her? Did that thought secretly please her?

One thing was certain: it was no prank. At least not by her. That meant he needed to explain himself, and fast. There was only one way he could think of to do that.

"There's something I need to show you," he announced.

"What is it?"

"It's in the basement," Wilbur declared with new resolve. The words sounded odd as he spoke them.

"I'm busy," Sarah replied, before turning away.

Was she reading something into his words? Maybe she thought it was a game or that he was in the mood. Or maybe she wanted it to be a game, and he had to play it. It vexed him that he did not know how.

"No, I'm serious," he persisted. "There's something I need to show you."

This time, when Sarah turned she looked him over. Was he supposed to say something, do something? It had been a long time since he had done anything.

"That's your space. There's a reason for that," she replied after a considered pause.

That was the arrangement, the treaty. It wasn't the only one, but an important one. And it served its purpose. Wilbur was certain that such treaties formed the skeleton of any successful marriage, though whether as cranium or toe he could not say. All he knew was that some semblance of balance had been achieved. A life forged with a stranger, but a stranger who knew him slightly better than other strangers and whom he once had fancied for reasons beyond recollection. He wondered whether she felt the same way. Perhaps that was what made it work — a commonality of thought, whatever that thought happened to be.

Nonetheless, he needed to break that treaty. Just this once.

"But I'm in *your* space right now," he countered.

"So you are." The cold glance and colder words made clear that his gambit had failed. Sometimes Wilbur wondered whether Sarah preferred him in the basement. He could not remember whose idea the agreement had been. Another approach was needed.

"I'm sorry. I just wanted to talk to you," he replied as sweetly as he could. He looked at his feet. "I missed you."

Sarah's face softened a little. It wasn't an act, and he keenly felt the words as he said them. He did miss her but was ashamed of such weakness and afraid of the rebuke it ordinarily would draw.

He remembered the crate and suddenly felt more confident. Surely she could not disapprove of being importuned about such an important thing. A thing large and unknown and sitting directly beneath her kitchen. It made him wonder about the thousands of miles of other unknown things beneath them.

"I value our spaces," he reassured her. "But there is something important I need to show you. It's okay to come into the basement if I ask you."

This seemed to catch Sarah off-guard. A momentary flash of anger crossed her face, making clear that it was not a lack of permission which kept her from the basement. She contemplated his neck where the tie had been. Her expression cleared, and when she replied it was in her usual brushoff sing-song voice.

"But all your stuff is down there, and it's a big mess."

Was she scared of the basement? Of him? The thought unnerved Wilbur, but he couldn't dismiss the possibility.

"None of that matters," he insisted, almost unaware that his voice had grown firm. "There's something I really need to show you."

"I'm not coming down there," Sarah reiterated, her voice now sour. There was a note of finality to it. Wilbur had heard this note of finality many times, which made it feel less final. Or perhaps it had been final the first time, and everything after didn't count.

—◦•◦—

After dinner, and as Sarah began to clear the table, Wilbur decided on a different approach.

"Hon, about the delivery," he began. The look she shot him made it clear her feelings had not changed.

He hurried to complete the thought before she did so for him. Her completion would be less charitable.

"You don't want to look in the basement."

Stony stare.

"So, I'll have to tell you instead."

"Tell me what?" Her patience clearly remained thin, but her voice was less icy. If anything there was a note of weariness in it. Maybe she just needed some sleep, and Wilbur was tempted to leave the matter until tomorrow.

"The crate in the basement."

She stared at him. "Crate?"

"There is a big crate in the basement."

"What crate?"

"I'm not sure," he replied. "I thought you may know."

"Why would I know?"

"I thought that maybe you…" He had to step gently and wasn't quite sure how to phrase this. The only certainty was that stammering would make things worse.

Sarah's eyes narrowed, and Wilbur settled for a hasty "Who delivered it?". He slumped into his chair, timidly glancing up to see whether Sarah had registered the question.

Her expression relaxed a little. Very little. "Some deliverymen."

"How—" he began, but she had vanished into the kitchen, and he had to wait until she returned for the remaining plates.

"But how did they get the crate down there?"

Sarah gawked at him as if he were a child. "That's what deliverymen do." She fixed his eyes. "Why are you making such a fuss about this? It's not the first time we've had something delivered."

Why *was* he making such a fuss? It took a moment before he remembered. "Never something this big," he explained. "It just seems strange. Did you see them do it?"

"What is this, an interrogation?" Sarah snapped. "You know what *is* strange? Your blue tie."

"That wasn't intentional," he protested.

"No doubt."

Did she think he *wanted* to wear such a thing? The quiet contempt of this insinuation rankled more than any of his wife's complaints, and Wilbur felt his temper rise.

"Well you were the one vacuuming on a Wednesday," he countered.

The retort visibly flustered Sarah, though he couldn't be sure whether it was his tone or the allegation. She soon recomposed herself, and her eyes had a cold glint to them. Wilbur immediately regretted his temerity.

"I'm sorry," he offered. "I didn't mean to sound critical. I just need to figure out how it got into the basement."

"Then figure it out."

"But didn't you see anything?" he pleaded. "Surely, you must be curious how it appeared there."

"I don't know and I don't care," Sarah grumbled.

"They said they had something to deliver. I told them to leave it where they could. I didn't watch them every step of the way."

Or any, apparently. Wilbur was disturbed by Sarah's cavalier disregard for their security. Did she leave workers unsupervised all the time? What else did she do when they were there? He wasn't so foolish as to voice this concern, though. Especially after his protestation of not being critical.

His thoughts were interrupted by Sarah's voice. She apparently hadn't finished with him. Or maybe she had finished with him years ago and just hadn't bothered to say anything.

"If you don't like the way I do things, feel free to do them yourself, mister."

For a moment, Sarah seemed on the verge of slamming down the plates. Wilbur cringed at the thought of buying new ones.

"I didn't mean that," he assured her. "It's just so ... big."

"Well, you'll have to deal with it."

When Sarah returned from the kitchen, Wilbur tried to propitiate her through small compliments and gestures, the things which always worked. She was too smart to be unaware of this, and Wilbur suspected she intentionally allowed herself to be placated. Maybe she got angry so she *could* be placated. He didn't pretend to know. What he did know was that wine helped. A little wine. Too much and he'd end up sleeping in the car.

But there remained the inescapable. He dreaded raising it again, but there was no avoiding the issue. When Sarah appeared sufficiently mollified, he gritted his teeth and broached the subject.

"It's not mine."

"What's not?" Sarah replied, her thoughts evidently elsewhere.

"The crate."

"Enough about your crate," she groaned.

"There's no way it could be mine," Wilbur persisted.

Sarah just shrugged. "So you've said." Did she not believe him, or simply not care? Well, she had to care. It affected her too.

"We'll have to return it," he announced.

Sarah stood, knocking her chair back from the table and almost upsetting her glass. Wilbur couldn't tell whether she truly was angry or just a bit tipsy.

"*You'll* have to return it." Her tone brooked no argument.

"But how?" he protested. A fiery silence filled the room.

"I'll deal with it, hon," Wilbur promised. Instead of sounding like a favor, the words emerged a servile rasp which lingered long after.

Sarah gave him a withering glare before starting up the stairs. "See that you do."

She stopped halfway and looked at him with something resembling pity. "Why don't you try opening it? Maybe something inside will tell you."

Wilbur stared at his wife, unsure what to make of her sudden encouragement.

"And we better not waste money on this," she called out before the bedroom door clicked shut.

When Wilbur returned to the basement, it was with newfound purpose. He had *permission*. If Sarah said something was ok, then it was ok. He would open the crate and find out what was inside. Assuming that's what she meant by "it".

The crate was even more impressive on close examination. There were symbols carved into the wood, but they didn't resemble any language Wilbur recognized. That struck him as strange. Who would carve information on a wood crate? Crates were disposable, and this clearly had been done with great care. Containers often were stamped with basic transport instructions, but the real delivery information usually appeared on a bill of lading. A bill of lading! That was what he needed. Surely, one of those had accompanied the box. He hoped he wouldn't need to actually open the crate. It looked like it would take a lot of effort.

Wilbur was about to ask his wife but caught himself. Why bother her? She clearly didn't know anything. He realized this was an absurd excuse but accepted it without hesitation. He did not relish challenging Sarah's reticence on the subject. This created a dilemma. How could he return the crate if there was no record of the sender or intended recipient or delivery company? Wilbur didn't even know how they got the thing in the basement.

Why *was* Sarah so reticent? No, not reticent. Downright irascible. This was a minor thing, a mere inconvenience which probably was nobody's fault. Yet it drew such a strong reaction. She always had a temper but rarely applied it so liberally. Was she mad about something else? Maybe the pressure had been building, and this was the release. Was it his tie?

Maybe she needed an emotional diaper, he grumbled to himself. Well, diapers *were* part of the bigger problem. He at least knew that much. Maybe they were the whole problem, but that felt like wishful thinking. A child wouldn't change who they were. It just would create new problems they would deal with the same way. Or worse.

But it was a moot point. A child was not to be. He knew Sarah secretly blamed him. The doctors never determined where the fault lay, or maybe just chose not to say. It didn't matter. It had to be his fault. It always was, and always would be. Maybe she was upset that the wrong thing had been delivered: a box instead of a baby.

Elegant as it was, the exterior of the crate furnished no clue to its provenance. Wilbur decided he had no choice but to open the damned thing. As Sarah had suggested, maybe there would be something revealing inside. He felt certain there would be. How could there not? Though the sender plausibly could have declined to attach an external bill of lading to preserve privacy or avoid advertising the contents, what decent reason could they have to omit such paperwork altogether? Maybe there was an indecent reason. What if the contents were dangerous or booby-trapped, designed to destroy its recipient but somehow delivered to the wrong victim. This sounded like the plot from a bad television show, and Wilbur decided to treat it as such.

He would be careful when opening the thing,

and that would be enough. There were a lot easier ways to harm somebody than by delivering a huge crate to their basement. Or so he surmised, having little practical knowledge of such matters. He would open the crate and learn something useful. The sender or intended recipient or delivery company. All he needed was some point of contact, any point of contact.

Wilbur was by no means a natural detective, nor was he inclined to imagine himself one. Despite a taste for books featuring such characters, he never pined for a life of danger. He couldn't understand people who did, and there were plenty. They'd tell him all the things they wished they were or wished to be. Those things always sounded dreadfully unpleasant, and their appeal eluded Wilbur. He enjoyed reading of such characters precisely to relish *not* being one. It helped him better appreciate the life he had and the many lives he did not. If people were so eager to be something else, why didn't they just *be* it?

Now Wilbur was forced to be one of those characters, and this did not please him. Why couldn't it have happened to the people who wanted such things? Maybe they would be happy. At worst, they would be deservedly unhappy. Shown the folly of such dreams, perhaps they would adopt Wilbur's pragmatism. It was important to understand that dreams were just dreams, otherwise they wouldn't be dreams. This was no dream.

The prospect of opening the box inspired a certain dread. It seemed a sin, irrevocable and beyond grace, like unwrapping a gift meant for somebody else. There was a finality to it. What if the contents spilled out, and he couldn't put them back? What if they broke? Wilbur was sorely tempted to plead with Sarah for any tidbit of information, anything which would remove the need to open it.

A deep fear kept him from doing so. He had left her annoyed but not angry. She even had offered advice, which meant there was no real rift. He would not trouble those waters further if at all possible.

He knew this equivocation would seem laughable to others, but the consequences were real enough to him. Wilbur had to live with Sarah, and she with him. Over the years they had established a fragile equilibrium. It was easy to disturb and laborious to restore. The ripples could last for years, and she never forgot. Anything.

In each argument, his past transgressions were revived, embellished, savored. He admired this gift of hers, even as he suffered from it. To what heights Sarah could have soared had her memory truly been perfect, transcending the minutiae of their relationship. But Wilbur had learned over the years that it failed on both counts. Her memory was transformative rather than eidetic.

When they were young, Wilbur had assumed the transformations were intentional. That she was acutely aware how pale and porous his own memory was, and could assert her version with impunity. He inevitably acquiesced to that version, absorbed it, made it his own.

With time, he came to recognize that the alterations weren't intentional or manipulative. This simply was how Sarah's mind worked. Those transformed memories were as true to her as the reality they replaced. They *were* her reality.

This understanding came with a certain measure of guilt. Another thing he had learned about Sarah was that there was no deceit in the woman. He was ashamed to have thought such a thing of her, to have mistrusted the woman he professed to love.

By what means or to what end her memories were transformed remained a mystery, but they were, and that was how she saw the world. It was this more than Sarah's occasional fire and fury which terrified Wilbur. Perhaps the machinery moved in its own time and by its own will and had nothing to do with him, but he would not take that chance.

Every time he upset his wife, Wilbur imperiled not just her feelings toward the present him but her memories of their past together. He was at the mercy of a temperamental time traveler, one who never would realize anything had changed or how much they both lost as a result. He wondered whether he too had such a defect, if defect it was. What secrets had Sarah discovered about *him* over the years, and were they equally incommunicable?

Most of all, he could not help wondering why she rewrote her memories. Had he fallen so short of her hopes, so despoiled her dreams, that she had to reinvent the past? If so, why hadn't she created a grander fiction for him? Wouldn't it be better to dream of the prince who grew feeble than the peasant she mistook for a prince? Diminishing the past to explain the present seemed pointless. But the consequences were real. He would not chance having the past diminished just for some convenience in the present. Opening the crate was the less perilous choice.

The crate proved easy to open. The keys not only turned in the locks, but their action was reassuringly smooth. Each lock popped open with a gratifying and unequivocal click. The latches released with little effort, and Wilbur instinctively recoiled. He did this less from fear of what was in the crate than that it would tumble onto him.

The side panel gently sank to the floor, its descent controlled by a small hydraulic cylinder. Wilbur realized how careless it had been to confine his concern to the contents rather than the crate itself. Had it just fallen open, the heavy wooden side panel could have crushed his feet. In fact, by instinctively springing back he had almost ensured it would.

Wilbur was grateful the thing had been carefully constructed. Carefully constructed was an understatement. The box had been over-engineered to a fault and looked well-nigh indestructible. It probably would survive long after the house crumbled around it. He remembered his promise to Sarah. It was his job to make sure that didn't happen.

Well-built though the crate may be, his safety could not be taken for granted. Wilbur had been lucky, and next time he might not be so fortunate. He felt queasy at the thought and resolved to be more cautious going forward.

The sudden realization that the box could be on its side occasioned another brief panic. What if something huge rolled out? He tried to step back but had nowhere to go. He took a deep breath. It was unlikely that deliverymen who showed enough ingenuity to get the box in the basement would neglect to orient it properly. That probably was what those carved symbols indicated.

Now that his thoughts returned to the delivery itself, other peculiarities began to emerge. Before opening the box, he had inspected every inch of the path to the basement. Aside from trying to discover how the deliverymen brought it in, he wanted to confirm they hadn't done any damage. To Wilbur's disbelief, there wasn't a single visible scuff mark.

But that was not all. Wilbur was no stranger to moving boxes. His first job out of school had been in a warehouse. Back then, he pushed the limits on a daily basis. In hindsight, it was foolish. They had forklifts and trucks, and there was no need for such physical exertion. Others had seemed amused by his superfluous effort, maybe even annoyed. Wilbur suspected that many of his present day aches and pains could be traced to that summer. Almost every injury he'd seen at work or the gym (back when he still went) had involved someone showing off.

Whatever his youthful excesses, Wilbur had developed a keen sense of heavy objects. He could estimate the weight of almost anything from a few small tugs. He even could guess an item's composition by the way it reacted. Every crate he had encountered, every box, every thing — even a car — shifted slightly when he really put his weight into it. The crate did not.

Wilbur gauged this before opening it. His efforts started gentle and grew in force. He didn't expect to lift an object of that size — the wood alone was solid enough to make it quite heavy — but he at least should have been able to budge it. He pushed and pulled and tried to tilt the crate but couldn't move it in the slightest. It was an odd feeling, like pressing against a mountain he didn't know was there. Even the wood didn't deform the way wood usually did. Wilbur never had seen anything like it. It felt wrong.

Something this heavy easily would have collapsed the stairs on the way down. They were ordinary wooden planks and creaked under Wilbur's weight. How they remained intact bothered him only slightly less than how an object that size got through the doorway or how anyone could carry it.

These mysteries fueled Wilbur's anxiety, and when it came time to open the crate he was a bundle of nerves. He blamed those nerves for his carelessness. It had turned out all right, though not by his doing. But none of this was by his doing.

Eyeing the now-open crate from the safety of one end, Wilbur waited a minute. If something inside was unstable or shifting, he would hear it. Satisfied that nothing would fall out, Wilbur finally looked inside. The interior was filled with hay-like packing material. He gingerly reached around the side and grabbed a tuft of the stuff. The material had the consistency of dense cotton candy. It felt soft, almost pleasant.

Only when he glanced down did Wilbur spot the blood. He dropped the material, which landed with an improbable thud. A nearby towel helped staunch the bleeding. To his surprise, there wasn't much actual blood. His hand looked like it had been shredded, but no longer bled. Wilbur cursed his carelessness. As he rushed up the stairs, he realized there was no pain.

Chapter 2

"Did you get rid of it?" Sarah called out as Wilbur dashed past the kitchen into the bathroom.

Did she really expect him to be done already? He ignored her and washed his hand thoroughly before applying alcohol. The intensity of the sting caught him off guard, and he forced himself to look at the hand.

Wilbur gave a sigh of relief. The hand was almost undamaged. Mingled blood from countless tiny abrasions had created the illusion of pulverized flesh. Once clean, what remained was little worse than a rash. Wilbur's relief immediately gave way to a new concern. What exactly was in the packing material? Was it poisonous? Would he get some nasty disease?

He realized there was nothing to be done at the moment. Maybe he would ask his doctor the next day, just to be sure. He briefly considered bringing a clump of the material, but something told him not to. Besides, what would a doctor know about materials?

"I'm working on it," Wilbur announced on his way back to the basement.

He donned a pair of work gloves, taking care not to aggravate the injured hand. Gently reaching into the crate, he retrieved some of the material. It didn't seem fine or fibrous enough to penetrate the gloves. Nevertheless he handled the first few tufts with great care, inspecting his hands every minute or two. Once satisfied that the gloves were adequate, Wilbur grew swifter and more confident. He deposited the material into large black lawn bags.

By now, Wilbur was less concerned with protecting himself from the material than keeping it intact. The stuff probably was hard to come by and could cost a lot. He was certain he would have to pay if any was missing.

Wilbur couldn't readily access more than a third of the interior from the open panel, nor did he wish to. The less he removed now, the less he'd have to put back later. He just needed to see what the box held, aside from abrasive cotton candy. Hopefully, he would find some clue to the true owner. Maybe even a manifest.

The more he dug, the less likely this seemed. It quickly became clear that the interior wasn't just protective wadding around something small and fragile. It had structure. There was a hefty metal framework holding the payload in place. This made sense, now that he thought about it. Wood and wadding couldn't support something so heavy. There had to be infrastructure to distribute the weight.

Metal plates lined the inside of the box, including the open panel. They were painted to match the wood, which probably was why he hadn't noticed them at first. Thick steel poles emanated from the corners of the crate, converging on a set of large rings which cradled an oblong object.

From Wilbur's constrained vantage point it was difficult to make out more. He was tempted to unlock the other side but preferred not to unless necessary. It would mean more work and risk. Just because he got away with opening the first panel did not mean the crate would allow an easy second. Perhaps it wasn't designed to have both sides open at the same time.

Wilbur continued digging. By now, the object's shape was discernible. It resembled a small submarine. To reach the remaining material, Wilbur was forced to partially squat into the newly excavated cavity. If the object dislodged now, he would lose more than a limb. He worked quickly, doing his best to avoid contact with any remaining packing material.

A cramped hour passed before he felt he had made sufficient progress, though it was too dark inside to tell. Wilbur carefully extricated himself from the cavity. Every bit of his body ached, and he hoped it was nothing more than muscle soreness. After some ineffectual stretching, he trained his flashlight on the interior.

A big, fat bomb peered back at him. It looked just like something out of a television show: a squat, round torpedo. In fact, the thing seemed so stereotypical that Wilbur had a difficult time believing it was real. Was this some sort of joke? If so, it was in terrible taste.

Wilbur had heard of people finding such things in fields or buried beneath buildings. Most were duds, but some weren't. Until now, he had given scant thought to the crate's contents. The thing had been a nuisance not a threat, its innards only of interest in potentially furnishing a clue to its rightful owner. No longer. Those contents now assumed a relevance all their own.

A tingling crept up his spine, a sense of acute peril. He wanted to run as far from the thing as possible. Maybe he even would take Sarah.

Wilbur regained control of himself. If the thing could harm him, it probably would have already. But this wasn't enough to put him at ease. Even if it wasn't dangerous, he didn't know that for sure. Who needed such a thing in their basement, under their very feet? A thing of uncertain nature and functionality.

A collector! The owner had to be a collector. Wilbur breathed a sigh of relief. It *was* a dud, a war relic. Only a collector would want such a thing. It all made sense now. That would explain the enigmatic delivery, the lack of information on the crate. A collector wouldn't be deterred by prosaic legality. Maybe the odd packing material was designed to thwart detection.

Collectors may be rich and eccentric, but they wouldn't compromise their own safety. They would not take delivery of a live device. For the briefest of moments, Wilbur wondered whether he was a guinea pig. Maybe this was how they tested whether it was live. If nothing happened, whoops wrong address – thanks for babysitting it – sorry for the trouble.

But something spoke against this. They'd need to give the thing freedom of movement. It would have to be able to roll and bounce and bump. Otherwise, how would they know whether it was inert or just hadn't been whacked hard enough. The object was too firmly secured for such a test. It had no freedom of movement at all.

The owner was a collector, and this just was an innocent mistake after all. A misdelivery. Such things must occur all the time. Just never to Wilbur. Well, it hadn't been delivered *to* Wilbur. He just happened to live where it ended up.

But something still didn't feel right. The object was sleek and modern, and its surface gleamed under the flashlight. It didn't look like something which had been dug up. Wilbur imagined it would take a great deal of painstaking restoration to attain such a state. Would a collector go to such lengths? Would they want to? Didn't that sort prefer their artifacts — what was the word the galleries used — "authentic"? They would want it authentic. They'd probably demand a certificate of authenticity. This thing was not authentic.

Nor did the object resemble anything from the war. Not that Wilbur was intimately familiar with such devices, old or new. But the pictures he'd seen in magazines or documentary reels or even television shows — they all looked different. For one thing, they were fatter. And the metal was flimsier, hastily bolted together for immediate use. This device was precisely-machined, a thing of beauty. It seemed impractically solid. Did they all look that way new?

But it wasn't just that. Those old bombs were shaped differently. They had few fins, and those were fixed. This device had many, visibly jointed. There also was a little window on the side. What could that possibly be for? Wilbur examined it closely, but could see nothing inside. Just grey.

What bothered him was *how* new the thing seemed. Factory-fresh. It was an intuition from his warehouse days. Wilbur could tell from the smell and the many little signs his flashlight revealed. Tiny bits of lubricant, small strips of metal threading, shavings of plastic that never got washed away. These were things one saw fresh off the factory floor. They said a car was new until the first time a mechanic's wrench touched it. No mechanic's wrench had touched this thing.

Every instinct told Wilbur to repack the crate. He did not.

Wilbur surveyed the space with mixed feelings. Completing one unpleasant task had created another. Large black bags occupied every inch of table along the walls. Ill-lit before, the room now was downright sepulchral.

Unpacking the entire crate had made him uneasy. He was beyond the safety of harbor. Would he be able to repack all this? It would be impossible to do right. The legitimate owner would know and demand an explanation. Was Wilbur committing a crime? What would he say to the owner? He would be hard put to justify his actions. Sure, he had to open the crate to find the bill of lading. But did he really have to unpack everything? It would strike people as questionable. Any hope of remaining unsullied by the affair had vanished.

Nor could Wilbur deny his own fault in this. Curiosity had whittled his resolve and overcome his qualms, strong as they were. His success opening the first side didn't help either. Aside from bestowing a certain confidence, it had revealed enough of the interior to whet his curiosity.

Wilbur had unlocked and lowered the second side panel with much less trepidation than the first, and perhaps less than prudence demanded. Nothing bad happened. As the interior was exposed, Wilbur grew more deft at maneuvering in the space. The support structure clearly was over-engineered. Nothing the size of the device could be heavy enough to bend those steel rings and rods. But the infrastructure wasn't the only such oddity. The wood panels appeared to do little other than contain the wadding and protect everything from the elements. They seemed needlessly solid for such banal purpose.

The bags he filled with packing material were improbably heavy as well. Wilbur had discovered this the hard way. The individual tufts felt light because they were uncompressed, but the material quickly grew dense when squeezed. It was an odd sensation, almost like packing steel wool to produce steel. The first bag simply burst when he tried to lift it.

Though frustrated, Wilbur took this in stride. In hindsight, it was a blessing. If the bag hadn't burst, Wilbur probably would have injured himself moving such a heavy thing. The lesson was learned. He placed subsequent bags on the tables while still empty and filled them only half-way. As the bags multiplied, he grew concerned about their cumulative weight. The side tables had numerous four-by-four legs, tightly spaced, but he couldn't shake the worry that these wouldn't be enough. He hoped there would be some warning before anything collapsed, but, despite a few disconcerting creaks as the last bags were filled, the tables held.

The amount of packing material was unexpected. Wilbur wondered whether it had been compressed in the crate and expanded only when he removed it. The prospect of repacking grew even more daunting. How would he compress all the material to get it back in? This gave rise to another question. Was the packing material responsible for the majority of the crate's original weight?

He couldn't imagine his tables supporting the weight of that immovable whole. The support structure looked like solid steel, which had to weigh a lot too. And the wood box. The object itself was too small to be very heavy. Unless it was solid steel. But who would go to such trouble to deliver some steel? As a quick test, he put his shoulder against one of the unopened sides. The crate didn't budge. However much the wadding weighed, what remained weighed more.

The rest of the excavation revealed nothing new about the device but did furnish two important discoveries. A second, smaller object was secreted in the packing material and remained hidden until nearly the last wad had been removed. In fact, Wilbur would have missed it altogether had he not felt an odd lump.

This lump turned out to be a small box with a transparent lid. Beneath the lid was a large red button, and it didn't take much imagination to guess what *that* was for. When Wilbur tapped the lid, he was greeted with a thin, hollow sound. It wasn't made of glass or quartz or anything he could think of. In fact, the box was as improbably light as the crate was heavy. This puzzled Wilbur almost as much as everything else, one more mystery to add to his trove.

In light of this discovery, Wilbur was tempted to sift through the previously unpacked material to see what else he may have overlooked. The thought depressed him. He had noticed the lump, so it stood to reason he probably would have noticed anything else. And he always could look later, if need be.

The second discovery was more serendipitous still. Even when the packing material had been removed, Wilbur could find no paperwork. He developed a sneaking suspicion it was attached to the bottom of the crate. Given how heavy the thing was, it would be impossible to get at. For the information he desperately sought to be close at hand but inaccessible would be more frustrating than if it was altogether absent.

Wilbur was about to call it a day but decided to have one last look inside. While excavating, he always had kept his head outside the crate. This involved some creative contortion at times and probably contributed to his aches and pains. It also made visual inspection of the interior more difficult.

The precaution stemmed from concern about the packing material rather than any fear of collapse. The last thing he needed was to shred his face or get bits of the abrasive stuff in his eyes or trek it through the house. By now most of the wadding had been removed, but some stray tufts still lingered. There was no reason to relax his discipline, and he even planned to remove his clothes and wash his hair afterward for good measure.

Wilbur stuck his head inside the crate. Whether he simply was being absentminded or this was an act of defiance or self-harm was unclear. Nor did he ever reflect on it. The discovery pushed everything from his mind. Something was stuck on the roof's underbelly. With a gentle tug, he dislodged a small booklet.

It was difficult to sleep.

The booklet had been infuriatingly imprecise in most places and impenetrably technical in the rest. Somehow Wilbur was meant to assemble its information into a coherent whole, and this was no recipe for a peaceful slumber. Not that peaceful slumber was the norm.

Sarah's presence didn't help. If not praise, he had expected some small acknowledgment of his effort after detailing his progress to her. Instead, he had gotten an earful for creating a mess in the basement. After that, she barely spoke a word before bed. What her silence failed to say, her face did. Now she lay inches from him, radiating resentment even in sleep.

Wilbur would have liked to study the book a bit more before bed, but Sarah had no patience for such things. Their relationship had certain unspoken rules, rules he had learned at great cost over the years. Of all those rules, this was one of the most inviolable.

She expected him next to her every night, all night. There was a price to deviating from this, and it was high. Nor could he wait until she was asleep and then slip away. She knew if he left for more than a few minutes, though he was uncertain how. Maybe the motion woke her or maybe, ever vigilant, she didn't really sleep. But how or why she knew didn't matter, only that she did. Sarah always went to bed at the same time and arose at the same time. Which meant Wilbur did too.

He had grown accustomed to this and usually did not mind. He even found it comforting. But on occasion it was a source of great frustration. At such times, he wondered why it was so important to her. All they did was sleep, nothing more. Was night the only time she could stand him, the only true peace in their relationship? Wilbur wondered what he was like in her dreams, if he even made the cut.

Or did she mistrust him? Perhaps she required constant proof of his fidelity. Or maybe he was her sentry, allowing her to rest while he kept the world at bay. Wilbur preferred to believe she needed him, if only while they inhabited different worlds. Perhaps she just needed somebody next to her, and he happened to be at hand. But even this would mean he was somebody, rather than nobody. That would offer some comfort, however small.

All Wilbur knew was that he did not mind, except when he did. Like now. It was doubly unfair. He would suffer just so she knew he was filling the proper space in bed. He would lay there listless all night, go to work exhausted, drag all day, and return miserable and tired. Because of her. Then she would complain that he hadn't taken care of the crate yet. Wilbur sensed he was being unjust to Sarah, but he couldn't help feeling irritated. He would have to wait a whole day before getting back to the little book.

The next day, Wilbur called in sick.

—●—

At first, Wilbur had high hopes for the booklet. Surely, such a thick trove of information had the answers he sought. But its heft was deceptive. The book was divided into twenty sections, each in a different language. He recognized a few, but the rest were gratingly unfamiliar. Some even felt obscene, and one made him physically nauseous.

The English section only was ten pages long, the print was large, and much of the space was taken by pictures. A quick glance confirmed Wilbur's suspicion: those same pictures graced every section. He wondered why the author had bothered to duplicate them, but already knew the answer. It was a user manual.

The little English which did appear was broken and barely comprehensible. It obviously had been translated by someone who did not know the language well. This came as no surprise. In his professional capacity, Wilbur often encountered English translations of technical documents. There was a vast difference between the product of a true polyglot and that of an unmotivated local, and there were few true polyglots in the business. Even so, not all unmotivated locals were the same. Some produced utterly incomprehensible gibberish, while others produced slightly less incomprehensible gibberish.

There also were certain idiosyncrasies endemic to each region, and over the years Wilbur had come to recognize these. Though not a particularly useful skill, it sometimes impressed his coworkers. He often could identify the specific country of origin for a document, and always the general region of the world.

This time he could not. The errors followed none of the familiar patterns. They most closely resembled a Russian translation, yet deviated noticeably. Wilbur suspected a dialect, maybe from some outer province.

That was a disconcerting possibility. It would mean he had become entangled in some manner of espionage. Wilbur had no desire to become entangled in anything, least of all espionage. If the movies were any indication, such things never ended well.

But why would spies bother to translate the booklet into so many languages? A user manual usually was intended for customers. Many translations would seem to indicate a global market. It also spoke against a collector. What collectible came with a user manual?

Customers made more sense. The device was new and intended for sale, probably at auction. Or maybe there was more than one. Was this something that could be ordered through the mail? Wilbur felt like an interloper in some perverse underworld.

But who would buy something like this? The English-speaking countries all had their own armies and arms. There were German and Italian translations, but the same held for those countries. What made even less sense was that there was an English translation at all. Who but America could produce such a device? Had somebody obtained an American weapon? Wilbur did not want to guess how such a thing might be acquired. Maybe it had been misdelivered to them.

Regardless, somebody was selling the device. Devices? The more Wilbur thought about it, the more likely this seemed. A single device would have a single customer, which meant a single language. Or maybe the same device made its way around the world from owner to owner. That would be slower but less harmful than the other way it could travel.

If sales were a frequent occurrence, why hadn't he heard of them? He imagined it would be hard to keep such things secret. Maybe they weren't deemed newsworthy.

If it had been sold, why hadn't someone demanded money? The merchandise had been delivered, so payment would be expected. This worried Wilbur more than espionage. Would some violent goons seek to exact payment? Violent goons weren't known for their understanding. Even if they had the patience to hear him out and, against all odds, believed that it was an innocent mix-up, what then? They wouldn't just collect the device and apologize for the inconvenience.

If they didn't silence him outright, maybe they'd demand money for their trouble. Returns always involved a restocking fee. It may not be the whole amount, but it still would be an impossible sum. And they'd know it.

Wilbur doubted he'd even make it to that point. They'd likely consider him a problem and certainly wouldn't believe he knew nothing. It would be obvious that the crate had been opened. No matter how hard he tried, there would be no way to hide this. For all he knew, the thing had a tamper seal anyway. He probably had doomed himself the moment he touched that first latch. It didn't take much imagination to guess what would happen when they discovered this.

Even if he somehow managed to escape, what would the police think? Wilbur felt his stomach turn. What *would* they think? He had a giant bomb in his basement and was trying to decipher the manual. Even if they accepted that the delivery was a mistake, nobody would believe he was innocent. Not in the true sense of the word. *Was* he innocent?

He imagined Sarah being interrogated. She'd contend that she had no idea he was a traitor, a villain, a monster. She never would have married a traitor, a villain, a monster. He must have tricked her. That's what traitors, villains, and monsters did. She could see it clearly, now that she was free of his clutches. Then she'd recount the myriad ways he'd wronged her over the years. He just was a man of low moral fiber.

That's what they always said, the wives and friends and families. It wouldn't be Sarah's fault. She would say it because she believed it. And she *would* believe it. There would be no reason not to. The evidence was in the basement. She would realize that he must be those things and would remember him as always having been those things. The traitor, the villain, the monster.

Everyone would applaud her courage, her patriotism, her forbearance. Heaven knew what they'd do with him. He'd heard of a case where a man spent many years in jail for contempt because the judge refused to believe he didn't know the answer to a question. That would be a life sentence for Wilbur. They'd never believe he knew nothing.

There only was one thing to do. With a groan, he set about doing it.

It took only half as long to repack the crate as to unpack it. Wilbur felt a cloud lift as the last padlock snapped into place. Everything had been restored to the way it was, the way it should be. His foray into the world of — he still didn't know what world it was — well, another world, a worse world, had been erased.

He simply needed to report the crate, and somebody official would take it away. Nobody would blame him; he just was a good citizen doing his duty. There would be no reason for anyone to kill or interrogate him after that. Maybe he'd get a reward. And the damned thing would be out of his life.

Then he remembered the little box and user manual. They were in his bedroom. Why had he left them there? It was a foolish thing to do. They belonged in the basement. That way, he would have remembered to pack them. Come to think of it, why had he taken the little box upstairs at all? The booklet made sense, but why the box? He couldn't remember moving it, much less a reason for doing so.

Though the prospect of reopening the crate was unappealing, restoring the booklet and box would be a simple chore. All he had to do was clip the manual to an inside wall and wedge the little box into the packing material. He'd only need to open a single side panel, the work of a couple of minutes. Why not just get it over with?

Wilbur turned off the light and climbed the stairs. Tomorrow. He'd done enough today. He'd put them back tomorrow.

Chapter 3

The decision was not to be taken lightly, nor was it. No less than six hours of anguished dithering preceded the inevitable capitulation. Another two hours passed before Wilbur managed the resolve to move forward. However, doing so was complicated by a number of issues. For one thing, he had no idea whom to call. It had been easy to envision abstract "authorities," but now it wasn't immediately evident who those authorities were or where they were to be found.

Calling the police would be straightforward enough, but there was no telling how they would handle such a situation. It seemed likely they would overreact or misreact or react in a way which would involve pain and inconvenience and possibly death. As it was Wilbur's main object to avoid precisely those things, the police were not an option.

While spy novels and bad movies abounded with secret agencies to handle every manner of threat, Wilbur was at a loss to identify any real ones. This left the FBI. They were more likely to appreciate the nuances of the matter, though he couldn't be sure they wouldn't escalate things.

It wasn't a great option, but it was better than the alternatives. Wilbur could think of no other way to avoid placing himself (and Sarah) in dire peril or creating a public hazard. A public hazard? He felt a bit absurd worrying about such a thing. What could be a bigger public hazard than the one in his basement? It just wasn't a publicized hazard.

While revisiting his doubts for the umpteenth time, Wilbur finally had the sought-after burst of inspiration. Well, perhaps not "sought after." He didn't believe in such things, much less seeking them. Bursts of inspiration simply happened. To other people. And this was fine with Wilbur. He'd spent his life blissfully free of such unpleasant things as inspiration and had hoped to remain that way. Nor did he expect to find it even if he did seek it. Given how uncharitably providence had treated him so far, why would it lend a helping hand now? He simply had stumbled into inspiration. That was all.

The idea was simple: publicity could be a friend as well as an enemy. The best way to ensure his (and Sarah's) well-being would be to shine a big, bright light on everything. He just needed to alert the press as well as the FBI. Nothing untoward would happen beneath the unforgiving gaze of journalists. Better yet, this would do more than merely prevent immediate violence. His name would be known and his cause recognized. The government would have a hard time ushering him away to some secret dungeon once the cameras were gone. It also would keep other threats at bay. Who knew what sort of unsavory people were mixed up in this affair — or would seek to be. Thugs and thieves would think twice before attacking someone under such intense scrutiny.

Wilbur had read of a similar stratagem in a novel. A hapless criminal robbed some dangerous folk, and his only hope of safety lay in surrender to corrupt police. To avoid being shot, he invited all the local newspapers. Wilbur couldn't recall whether the fellow ended up dead or in prison. Neither prospect was particularly appealing.

But Wilbur was no thief. If anything, he was the victim. Who could blame someone for a mistaken delivery? And wasn't he doing the right thing by reporting it? He was being civic-minded. Nobody would fault someone for being civic-minded. Maybe they even would call him a hero. Wilbur felt a new twinge of panic. He didn't want to be called a hero. Being paraded on stage for a medal would be terrifying.

~•~

"That's stupid."

Sarah did not elaborate. She did add that she wanted no part in it. And that he'd better make sure she wasn't around when he did something so dumb.

When Wilbur tried to explain his reasoning, she cut him off.

"Why would you call anyone but the delivery company?"

This really riled Wilbur, and he decided he'd had enough. The situation was desperate. The least she could do was show a little support.

"Somebody didn't bother taking down their information," he snapped.

They were harsh words from a man who barely ever raised his voice. He could not recall having used such a tone with his wife … ever. Wilbur awaited the predictable consequence.

To his shock, Sarah did not grow furious or rebuke him or even storm out of the room. She just looked at him.

In some ways, he found this silence more unnerving. Wilbur doubted she would let such a thing pass. Not truly. She probably was filing it in the cavernous vault of grievances upon which their marriage was built. She would issue some parting cruelty, and hell would follow soon enough.

"Do what you want," she replied, then quietly left the room.

Relieved as he was at the civility of her response, Wilbur found its ambiguity disconcerting. What precisely did Sarah mean? What boundaries were circumscribed by "what you want"? Its latitude felt ominous, its responsibility oppressive. Wilbur had no notion how to figure out "what he wanted." After twenty-odd years of married life, he had forgotten what those words meant.

—•—

Daunting enough in itself, this sudden freedom was worsened by Wilbur's uncertainty whether it was real or imagined. In the end, he settled on telephoning three local news stations before alerting the FBI. Even this proved troublesome. He had no more idea how to contact the media that the authorities.

Wilbur spent several hours at the local library researching journalists. To his surprise Sarah helped. To his greater surprise, she did so without complaint.

Once again, Wilbur wondered whether he really knew his wife at all.

Preparatory work complete, all that remained was to compose a short statement. Something to stick to. Wilbur went through several drafts before landing on something which sounded right. Sarah helped with this as well, serving as the audience on which he rehearsed his little speech. His reading finally earned her approval, though it felt stilted to him. He decided to proceed anyway. His job wasn't to prepare speeches or deliver them. He was performing under duress, and the public would have to be satisfied with what limited skill he could bring to bear.

The next morning (it always was best, to his mind, to get a good night's sleep before embarking on a new venture), Wilbur lay out the script on the kitchen table. He felt tired and sore, having spent the night wide awake but motionless to avoid disturbing his wife. He wondered what sort of impression he would make in this state. It didn't matter. If he waited, the next day would be worse. He needed to get this done while he still had the resolve.

Unfortunately, it was Sunday. Wilbur hadn't considered whether the FBI would be open on a Sunday. Were the newspapers? Maybe criminals took Sundays off, or Sunday crimes were reported on Monday. He couldn't chance it. If nobody answered the phone, he wouldn't know whether they were ignoring him or just closed for the day. Calling once was difficult enough, and he doubted he had the fortitude to try twice.

After a listless day and another sleepless night, Monday morning finally arrived. Wilbur's jaw dropped when Sarah dutifully joined him for the call. She even smiled. For a fleeting moment, he entertained a terrible suspicion. Was she exulting in this? Maybe she saw it as a vehicle to be rid of him. What would she really say when questioned by the FBI?

Wilbur suddenly felt ashamed. She was on his side, supporting him, playing a proper wife. And *this* was how he repaid her? If they got through this, he promised to think better of her.

With Sarah there, his prospects felt less bleak. A vague hope of success was kindled. They practiced having Sarah stand next to him, smiling. It was a telephone call, but an impression needed to be conveyed. There also was no telling how quickly the FBI would respond, and they might not have time to compose themselves properly.

Having Sarah don an apron seemed a bit much, so they settled on a pleasant dress. Like those smiling politicians' wives on television. Nobody got shot by trigger-happy agents when a smiling wife was at their side.

Right before Wilbur picked up the phone, Sarah gave his hand an encouraging squeeze. It evoked an odd tenderness. Was she as afraid as he was? Wilbur had come to see her as a child sees a parent: unfathomable, all-knowing, easily annoyed. What if he was wrong? What if she was far more fragile than she let on? The idea seemed absurd. Sarah fragile? He felt sorry for the FBI agent who tried anything around her. That thought pleased him. He was glad to have her by his side.

With trepidation, Wilbur picked up the phone. Sarah's eyes clutched his, and he sensed a desperation he never had seen before.

"This cannot be undone," she warned. "Are we sure?"

Wilbur felt a surge of pride at the word "we". They were a team. He and his wife. Maybe he could love her. Again? Was it again, or at all? Wilbur was not sure, and now was not the time for such questions.

His newfound pride begat newfound confidence. He smiled.

"I'm sure."

~•~

The first number on their list was busy, and the second rang through. At the third news agency, someone picked up. He sounded very young.

"I'd like to speak with a reporter," Wilbur began.

"I'm a reporter," the man or boy or boy-pretending-to-be-a-man replied.

"Are you sure?" Wilbur asked without thinking.

"Why else would I be at a news agency?"

"Well, I have something to report," Wilbur continued, a little less sure whether he was doing the right thing. For some reason, he had envisioned a seasoned old man. Or maybe one of those hard-nosed journalist gals. This fellow sounded so young. Wilbur wondered whether he just was getting old. To an old man everyone sounded young.

There was a pause. "I think you have it backward," the boy replied.

"How so?"

"If I'm the reporter, shouldn't I be doing the reporting? If you report something, that makes you the reporter."

"Yes, I suppose," Wilbur conceded. It did make sense, after a fashion. "But I have something to report," he insisted.

"If you're a reporter, why do you need a reporter?"

Wilbur thought about this for a moment. "Is there somebody else I can speak with?"

"I'm sure there are many people you can speak with. I can't say whether you should speak with them, though."

"Can you put me through to one?"

"I just meant in general. I'm the only one here."

Wilbur was astonished. "The whole news agency is you?"

"For now. Everyone else arrives later."

Wilbur looked at the wall clock and groaned. In his anxiety, it hadn't occurred to him that nobody would be at work this early. After a hurried excuse, he hung up.

Sarah's expression demanded answers.

"Just an intern," he explained, trying to sound as nonchalant as possible.

"An intern?" she asked with an uncomprehending expression.

"It's too early." Wilbur waved at the clock.

Sarah glanced over. "I'll make some breakfast."

She quietly rose from the table, her face the usual picture of disdain.

Wilbur tried again two hours later. Sarah once again stood by his side, but this time it felt more literal and less figurative. There was no gentle squeeze of the hand, no "we". Was this what the politicians' wives were like, privately despising the partners they publicly extolled?

In retrospect, it should have come as no surprise that the press was uninterested. Who would believe such a claim from some random guy? He was a pathetic attention seeker, too inept to concoct a plausible fiction.

Wilbur ended up trying more than seventeen news outlets. Sarah's patience quickly waned, or perhaps she grew tired of the constant strain on her nerves. After the first few attempts she retired to the bedroom, occasionally asking whether he'd had any luck. Soon she didn't even bother with that.

Some people just hung up. Others indulged Wilbur but could not disguise their skepticism. A couple openly mocked him, but most were more subtle. They asked facetious questions, trying to draw him out — though it was unclear why.

One reporter exhibited keen interest in the story but soon launched into a narrative of his own struggles to expose a secret communist cabal in Alabama. Wilbur innocently marveled that there *were* any communists in Alabama, and the call did not end well.

Nor were journalists interested in the photographs Wilbur offered to send. He had borrowed a friend's

Instamatic and taken some nice ones despite the poor lighting. He even developed them himself, and was quite proud of the result. One person did ask for them, but Wilbur recognized the address as that of a local supermarket.

Only one reporter took the time to explain his indifference.

"Anyone can fake a photo," he pointed out. "How do I know it isn't just a toy you bought, or maybe a scale model. It is easy to build a replica."

"I don't think that would be easy to do," Wilbur protested.

The man snorted dismissively. "Nobody believes photos anymore. Photos lie. Only words tell the truth."

This didn't sound right to Wilbur, but he decided not to argue the point. Instead, he reiterated his invitation to see the device in person.

"I'm busy," the reported replied. "But even if I wasn't, I'd never set foot in a stranger's home. It's a matter of personal safety, you see."

"How do you investigate?" Wilbur wondered.

"That's easy," the man laughed. "I look things up on the internet. There are lots of people willing to go into strangers' basements. So I go on the internet and see what they say."

Wilbur saw a ray of hope in this. There *were* people who would be interested, and they were on this "internet". It sounded familiar and reminded him of something he did at work. Something he did a lot. But for some reason, he couldn't remember what.

"How do you find these people?" he asked.

"It's easy," the reporter explained. "You just go online and search."

Wilbur was unsure what this meant but hoped it would come to him at work. He seemed to know a lot more things there than here. Or different things, work things. They didn't have a purpose outside work, and he never brought them home with him.

Before he could ask any more questions, the man hung up.

Wilbur didn't want to wait until the next day at work. He probably would forget by then anyway. Finding a reporter was a home thing, and home things rarely made it to work. He needed to resolve the matter without delay.

There was no "internet" listed in the phone directory, and Sarah just shook her head when he asked about it. Wilbur decided the reporter had been speaking nonsense. It was just another form of rejection. He filed it with the rest and wondered why the man had taken time to explain things at all.

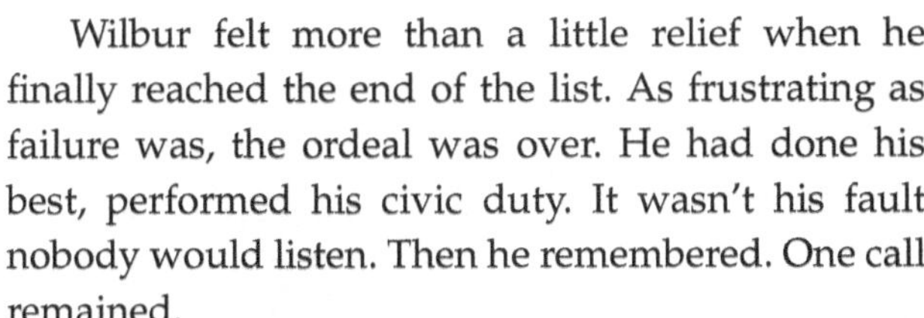

Wilbur felt more than a little relief when he finally reached the end of the list. As frustrating as failure was, the ordeal was over. He had done his best, performed his civic duty. It wasn't his fault nobody would listen. Then he remembered. One call remained.

Wilbur's stomach sank. He had become so obsessed with alerting the press that he forgot his actual purpose in doing so and why success was so important. It was to have been his insurance policy for this next call, the means of ensuring it did not end in disaster. Now there was no insurance, and Wilbur felt naked picking up the phone.

With a slow sense of foreboding, he dialed the number for the FBI. He deliberately did not summon Sarah before doing so. Much as Wilbur longed for her support — for anyone's support — it would be cruel to tell her.

She had grown accustomed to the calls, had lowered her guard. She thought they still were to journalists and carried no weight. As long as she did not know when the fateful call would be made, she could pretend it was in some indefinite future.

If he told her, that would change. She would know what was at stake and feel every inch of it. Wilbur did not want the guilt of imposing that on her. She did not need to know he was making *this* call, that there really was no turning back.

"Agent Smith," a man answered. Did they really answer the phone like that? Wilbur had expected a receptionist or maybe an intern. And was he really Agent Smith? It seemed so ... cliched. But the last thing Wilbur wanted was to start by insulting the man's name.

"Hi, I don't know if this is the right number ... " Wilbur began.

"Then why did you call it?"

"Um, I thought you may be the one I should talk to."

"You think I'm the right man, but you don't think you have the right number."

"I didn't say—"

"The man and number, we are the same. If you

call the number, you get the man. If you need the man, you call the number."

Wilbur did not know how to reply to this, so he went to the script.

"I have something to report."

"Then you want Agent Jones." The man hung up.

Wilbur gently returned the phone to its cradle, hoping Sarah wouldn't decide to inquire just then. He wasn't sure whether to laugh or cry. It was tempting to do both. Instead, he quietly reached for the phone. It rang. Wilbur almost leapt from his seat, then felt a burst of irritation. Now was not the time for some telemarketer. If Sarah heard the phone ring, she probably would come down. He quickly snatched the phone, before it could ring again.

"Agent Jones," a man announced. His voice sounded exactly like Agent Smith's.

Wilbur was at a loss for words.

"You have something to report?" the man prompted.

Wilbur instinctively went to the script.

"I have something to report," he repeated.

"I'm sorry, but I have no comment for reporters."

"Then why—"

"It would be impolite not to return a call," Agent Jones observed. "And against policy."

Wilbur's mind raced. He could not afford to squander this opportunity. What if "policy" required the man to hear him out? He decided to try.

"Please, I have something I need to report to you."

"We've already established that."

"But—"

"If you're reporting something, you're a reporter and I don't speak to reporters."

"It's important!" Wilbur blurted out.

"What's important?"

"This thing I need to report."

"I can't do your job for you, pal," Agent Jones admonished. "A reporter should know that sort of thing."

"I'm not a reporter!"

"You said you have something to report."

Wilbur decided to rephrase. "I need to tell you something."

"I'm not here to satisfy your needs. Just to help people in need."

"That's it! I'm a person in need."

"What sort of need?"

"I have" — Wilbur thought carefully — "a thing in the basement. It's very dangerous."

"Is that a threat?"

"No, I'm trying to tell you about it."

"That's the definition of a threat. It wouldn't do much good if you didn't tell me about it."

"It's not a threat!" Wilbur felt his temper rising. He had to take back control of the conversation.

"I'm trying to do my civic duty."

"By making threats?"

"No, by warning you of something dangerous. A device that was delivered to me."

"Truth be told, I don't mind all threats. If I make a threat then I don't mind it."

Wilbur felt dizzy. He blurted out what he had in the basement.

"Oh my."

Wilbur was taken aback by the tepid response. "That's it?" he asked.

"You expected more?"

Wilbur confessed that he had. "It's a pretty big public danger," he protested.

"It sounds like one. But we're stretched rather thin."

"You don't believe me."

"I can't comment on that, especially to a reporter."

"Please just listen. Millions of people are in danger."

Agent Jones laughed. "Now *there's* a threat."

"It's not a threat."

"Don't be modest. A bit melodramatic perhaps, but a quality threat."

"Can you please send someone?"

"Where?"

"My basement," Wilbur replied in a tone of exasperation.

"I'm afraid not."

"Why not?"

"Why would we?"

"That's where the danger is."

"It sounds like a place to avoid. I try not to put my people in danger."

"But lots of people are in danger," Wilbur argued.

"Then *they* should go into your basement. They're already in danger, so a little extra is no big deal."

Wilbur had no idea what to say, so he said nothing. He heard a click, then some other clicks, then a female voice say, "on line 2."

"Agent Smith."

Wilbur quietly hung up.

"Any luck?" Sarah called out.

"FBI says they're not interested."

"I told you," she replied, strolling into the room, hands on her hips. "Why would they be interested in somebody's delivery issue? Maybe you should start with the post office."

Chapter 4

"Why are you trying to get rid of it?" Erik asked before taking a big bite of his sandwich.

Once it became clear nobody official was interested in the device, Wilbur decided there was little point being secretive about it. Maybe if he was loose-lipped enough someone finally would take notice. There also was a certain security in this. They hardly could accuse him of hiding the thing if he told everyone about it.

Wilbur only had one friend, so "everyone" was Erik and being "loose-lipped" meant raising it during lunch. Sarah already knew as much as she cared to and had made it painfully clear what would happen if Wilbur were loose-lipped toward *her*.

Naturally, Erik was skeptical. Wilbur offered to show him the device, but he declined, explaining that he preferred to keep work friendships at work. If they started visiting one another's homes, it would be harder to backstab him. Wilbur had a good laugh at this but did not press the invitation.

Instead, he produced the user manual. Wilbur had deliberated quite a bit before bringing it to work. He was loathe to risk damaging the booklet but suspected it was his only means of convincing Erik.

Erik laughed. "Anyone can print a manual."

"Can they?" It seemed a daunting task, with fonts and diagrams and so many languages. Wilbur certainly did not have the equipment to print such a thing. He asked whether Erik did.

Erik shook his head. "No, I just go to the store for that sort of thing." He put out his hand. "Ok, let's see it."

Wilbur realized he was clutching the manual in his pocket and hoped he hadn't wrinkled it. He drew it out and gave a sigh of relief.

"It's the only one I have," he explained. "I need to keep it safe."

"Why don't you just photocopy it?" Erik suggested.

Wilbur scratched his head for a moment. "I didn't think of that."

It also hadn't occurred to him that Erik actually would want to see the book. Despite having brought the thing for this very purpose, he had hoped its mere presence would suffice and he would not be required to relinquish it. This made little sense on reflection. Who would believe a man just because he had a book? Lots of people had books. Liars had books. Books were to be trusted, not the people who owned them. And he didn't even own it.

He hesitantly relaxed his grip. Erik smiled and snatched the booklet from his hand, almost tearing a page. Wilbur cringed as his friend casually thumbed through it, then tossed it on the table. With a reproachful look, Wilbur retrieved the manual.

"I have to give this back," he complained, dabbing at a coffee stain.

"I told you to make a copy."

"They'll want what I was given."

Erik sat back. "Yeah, I suppose so. I'd want what

you were given."

"You do?"

"Would."

Wilbur put his head in his hands and sighed. "What should I do?"

"Well, there's another way of looking at it." Erik took a sip of coffee.

"What's that?"

"How do you know it wasn't meant for you?"

Wilbur thought for a moment. "I didn't order it."

Erik slid his coffee cup toward Wilbur. "You didn't order this either, yet here it is."

"You're giving it to me?"

With a wry expression, Erik grabbed back his cup. Some of the remaining coffee sloshed over the side, and Wilbur was glad the manual was safely back in his own hands.

"The point is ... " Erik began.

Wilbur leaned forward attentively, and this seemed to bother Erik. His voice grew impatient.

"The point is that our will doesn't affect the world. Especially in your case."

Wilbur gave an uneasy laugh.

"Look," Erik grinned. "Does the world deliver what you want?"

"Generally not."

"Definitely not. So why be surprised when it delivers what you don't want?"

Never since the crate arrived had Wilbur entertained the possibility that it was meant for him. That it was not a mistake. The thought bothered him. It would change everything. The reporters, the FBI, everyone ... they all would blame him. He *was* culpable. Was he? Wilbur felt certain he would be blamed, regardless. If he did not exist, the device never would have been delivered to him. Ergo, he was to blame.

～•～

"So what are you going to do with it?" Erik asked while chewing.

The words derailed Wilbur's train of thought, but he promptly embarked on a new one. When the device had not been his, he only considered what to do about it. Now he must consider what to do *with* it. He was back to square one. He shuddered to think how Sarah would react if it really was his. When she learned all their efforts had been pointless, that it was here to stay. Wilbur still didn't know whether it *was* meant for him. But the question was a good one. What would he do if it were?

"I don't know," he replied after a few moments. He felt a pang of guilt at making Erik wait for such an uninformative reply.

"I suppose not."

Suddenly Wilbur perked up. "What about you? What would you do?"

Erik pushed back his chair from the table. "Whoa, let's leave me out of this."

"Why not sell it?" he added after a few seconds.

"Sell it?"

"You give it to someone, and they give you money. People do it all the time. Any idea how much a thing like that would be worth?"

Wilbur shrugged. "I'm not sure."

"I see." Gears clearly were turning in Erik's head.

"But who would I sell it to?" Wilbur ventured after a few moments.

"No idea. Somebody bad, probably. I don't think good people would want such a thing. A terrorist maybe?"

"I wouldn't want a terrorist to have one. They could blow me up."

"*You* could blow you up."

The possibility hadn't truly registered before. Wilbur had been cognizant of the danger, but it felt abstract, theoretical. Now he couldn't shake a sense of very real and acute peril. How had he been so sanguine about this? He *could* blow himself up. Maybe. If the device even worked.

"Well, selling it probably would be a waste anyway," Erik declared.

"Why is that?" Just when Wilbur was coming to grips with the idea of selling it, the rug was pulled out. He wasn't even sure whether Erik was being serious. The man's flippant attitude was vexing.

"If you have something like this ..." Erik looked Wilbur hard in the eye. "If you truly have something like this, why not use it?"

"That would be horrible. Millions of people would die. Probably you too. And Sarah."

"Not like that," Erik replied with an impatient wave of the hand. "You could parlay it into world domination."

"I'm not sure how to do that. It's a one-shot deal, and everyone would know that."

"You probably could blackmail everyone or play off nations against one another. Think like an evil genius."

"How would an evil genius think?"

"How would I know? Maybe read a comic book."

Wilbur lay back in his chair and groaned. "What am I going to do, Erik?"

"Well, the first thing is to figure out exactly what it is and how it works. You'll need to know that."

"All I have is the manual." Wilbur eyed the visible coffee stain and frowned. "The deliverymen didn't leave a manifest."

"So what? Since when do you need a manifest to tell how something works?"

Wilbur sprang forward in his seat. "You're right. I can use the scientific method."

"Exactly," Erik replied, tapping the table for emphasis. "The scientific method."

"So how do I do that?"

"You need a scientist. They know all about the scientific method."

Wilbur pondered this a bit. "But I don't know any scientists."

"You do, but just don't know it." Erik gave a self-satisfied grin.

"You?"

"Do I look like a scientist?"

Wilbur was embarrassed for suggesting such a silly thing. Erik didn't have a white lab coat or clipboard. How could he be a scientist?

"But Sarah knows one," Erik continued.

"My wife knows a scientist?" Wilbur was astonished to hear this and equally astonished that Erik would be aware of such a thing.

"One of her bridge friends."

Wilbur raised an eyebrow.

"Greta Wendell-Kaufman."

The name rang a bell, but Wilbur couldn't place it.

Erik smiled. "Gal who wrote that famous book on how Dark Matter killed JFK."

"Sarah has that book on our coffee table. I had no idea she knew her."

"I don't think they're best friends," Erik explained. "But with these bridge gals you never can tell."

"How do you know all this?"

"Just common knowledge."

"Then why didn't I know it?"

"You're uncommon."

Wilbur jumped up.

"Hey, don't be like that," Erik called out. "It's not always bad to be uncommon."

"Thank you," Wilbur gushed, clasping his friend's hand before scurrying to the cafeteria door.

Erik sipped his coffee as the door slammed shut. "What about work?"

Chapter 5

Wilbur was loathe to ask anything of Sarah, least of all entangle her friend in his mess. It was tempting to imagine he had no choice, but he sensed the fallacy in this. What if Erik hadn't mentioned the scientist? If the "only alternative" was not an alternative would he have found another? Maybe he just was being complacent.

Wilbur racked his brain for a full day but could think of no better plan. This didn't entirely allay his concern. What if having a path deprived him of any compelling desperation and narrowed his vision to its vicinity? He decided it did not matter. The alternatives were immaterial if he could not see them. For better or worse, this was the course he was on.

That course was very different from his initial one. His priority had shifted from removing the device to understanding it. This change in perspective wasn't prompted by his complete failure so far, though that may have played a role. Rather, it was the result of hearing another opinion. The introduction of outside thoughts and a fleeting reprieve from the warped echoes of his own. Lost in his desire to be rid of the device, Wilbur had given scant consideration to how it worked. No longer. Erik had opened his eyes to the overarching importance of this question. At the very least, he needed to know *whether* it worked.

At first, Wilbur was wary of this newfound

curiosity. Did he want to know so he could be rid of the device, or so he could assume ownership? However, it was not long before he managed to dismiss such skepticism of his own motive. Or perhaps he simply decided it did not matter. The pursuit of such knowledge assumed cardinal significance, and it seemed unfathomable that he hadn't realized this from the start. How could he get rid of the thing without knowing what it was? That was nonsensical, an impossibility.

The easiest way to ascertain whether the device worked would be to ask an expert. Well, the second easiest way. Part of Wilbur was tempted to press the red button. Fortunately, it was a small part and not a very influential one. It was the part that other parts mostly told to shut-up during lunch or in meetings.

Nevertheless, Wilbur was glad the button was encased. That presented a barrier to impulse. It meant inconvenience, a moment's delay, time enough for the briefest reflection. How often had a moment's delay prevented some catastrophic impulse? Not often enough, he suspected. Was the happenstance of impulses what secretly guided the course of human affairs?

This raised a new concern, one which Wilbur took to heart. Until now, his impulses were of little import. At worst they could affect him and one or two other people, and they never actually did. He lacked the imagination for a dangerous impulse or the temerity to act on it. Proposing to Sarah was the closest he had come, and that only was on impulse because he lacked the guts to plan such a thing.

Now Wilbur had to adjust to a new reality.

The device could be real. It could be his. His impulses could matter. They could have catastrophic consequences. Could, could, could. The word bothered him. It would be nice to know for sure.

He decided to ask Sarah about her friend.

To Wilbur's immense relief, Sarah was not angered by the request. In fact, she didn't seem the least bit surprised. Her impatient nods and curt assent gave the distinct impression of someone who expected to be asked and just wanted to get it over with.

That made sense. Even if he didn't know about the scientist, she did. But why hadn't she mentioned her? It would have been a small thing, a useful thing. Perhaps Sarah did not want to involve her friend but would not refuse if asked. Wilbur suffered a pang of guilt, though he still felt they should have discussed the matter. Why was he dwelling on this? He had what he wanted, and without any lost skin. How often did *that* happen?

Sarah's precise reply had been "if it means I'll finally stop hearing about that damned package." She even wrote her friend's phone number on a slip of paper and handed it to him.

"Do you think, maybe you could ask ..." Wilbur began, but Sarah's expression eviscerated the question before it was out. He could not fault her for this. He had promised to take care of it himself, and she already was doing more than could be expected.

"Thank you, hon," he amended.

Sarah gave an inscrutable smile. All her smiles were inscrutable. Only her frowns were not.

Wilbur dreaded cold calls. This technically wasn't a cold call, but it was close enough to merit dread. It didn't help that the woman was Sarah's friend. Wilbur was certain every gaffe would find its way to his wife's ear, embellished and annotated. The two women would laugh at him over bridge or lunch or whatever it was they did together. What *did* they do?

It occurred to Wilbur that he knew very little about Sarah's private life. Until his conversation with Erik, he didn't even know she had a private life. Was Greta her only friend? Her best friend? A friend at all? It struck him as something which mattered, something a husband ought to know. What if this woman was Sarah's enemy? What if there were things he shouldn't tell her? How would he know the delicate interplay of their lives when he didn't even know Sarah *had* a life.

Wilbur picked up the phone. He would stick to the topic and say little else. Besides, he didn't know what this professor was like. Speaking to any professor was intimidating, and she was a famous one. Before he lost his courage, Wilbur dialed the number.

In the liminal moment between dialing and the ring, it took all of Wilbur's resolve not to hang up. Was it too late? Would she know he'd called if he hung up quickly? The first ring sounded. Then the second. Why was he this nervous about some academic? He hadn't felt nearly as anxious calling the FBI.

A female voice answered.

"Professor Wendell-Kaufman?" Wilbur stammered, before realizing the woman's voice sounded odd. It was not a professorial voice.

"Moooooom," the voice called out, muffled through gauze.

How was "Wendell-Kaufman" pronounced, Wilbur wondered as he waited. Was the hyphen silent?

"What." It was a different female voice. There was nothing listless about this one. Wilbur suddenly felt very shy.

"I'm a friend of … ," he began.

"My wife suggested I …" Third time would be the charm.

"I have something to ask you."

"Doesn't everyone."

"My wife gave me your number."

"My wife gave me yours."

Wilbur was taken aback, then realized it was a joke. Was it? He was unsure whether to laugh and did not.

"Um, ok."

"I jest. Who is your wife?"

"A friend of yours from bridge."

"I have lots of friends. And they all play bridge."

It seemed an odd boast for a professor.

"Um, Sarah."

"My name's not Sarah."

"Her name is Sarah."

"Are you sure? You don't sound sure."

Wilbur thought for a moment. "She's my wife. I'm sure her name is Sarah."

"If you say so."

"I do."

"What else do you plan to say?"

"What do you mean?"

"Well, I assume you didn't just call to tell me your wife's name."

"Right, that." Wilbur felt a wetness above his right eye and realized he was perspiring. There was nothing in easy reach, so he patted his eyebrow with a shirtsleeve.

"I have a device."

"What sort of device?"

"That's what I want to know."

"And you called because you think I would know."

"I hope so."

"You want advice about your device."

It sounded odd rolling off her tongue that way. Wilbur could not tell whether she was belittling him.

"Is that a euphemism?" Greta continued. "It better not be a euphemism. I don't like euphemisms."

"A euphemism?"

"I do not react well to euphemisms. That's not a euphemism, by the way."

"It's not—"

"You'll have to tell me more about this device," the professor demanded.

Wilbur related what he knew of the delivery and device, though he omitted his abortive attempts to report it. When he finished, there was a long silence before the professor finally replied.

"You've said plenty about the delivery but next

to nothing about the device itself. I can't very well tell you about it unless you give me something to go on."

"I think it's nuclear," Wilbur declared with a certainty which almost could be mistaken for confidence.

"Why do you think that?"

"It says so in the manual."

There was another pause. "Why do you need my advice if you have a manual?"

"I don't understand what the manual says or know whether it is true."

"That pretty much sums up history."

"What—"

"What don't you understand?"

This caught Wilbur off guard. In all his worry and preparation, he had not considered precisely what to ask. He just knew he needed help. What *did* he hope to learn? There was so much he did not understand. A better question would be what he did understand.

"What if you read me the bit you're having trouble with?" the professor prompted.

Wilbur thumbed through the manual for a few moments.

"Well?"

"Sorry, it's in several languages," he explained.

"I only speak English," she warned. "And a little bit of French. Not scientific French, mind you."

"It's not in French. Just English and some others."

"Read the English," she instructed.

Wilbur felt an inexplicable need to prove his

worth, to show he wasn't the buffoon she surely assumed he was. He looked for the English section.

"Here it is," he announced triumphantly. "Let's see—"

"Yes, let's." Was that sarcasm? It was hard to tell over the phone.

"Third order decay coupling ... cross-section for reabsorption ..."

No response. Wilbur waited a few moments. "Do you know what that means?"

"No idea."

Wilbur's spirits sank. He had assumed a famous professor would know everything. Now he sensed how absurd this was. Why should she know everything? *How* could she know everything? Maybe this was some obscure bit of engineering jargon or from an unrelated field. Wilbur had no idea whether they were words a physicist should know. Clearly, they were not. What would he do now? His thoughts were interrupted by the professor.

"I don't have time for this," she snapped, suddenly impatient. "I'll give you a grad student for a day."

Wilbur felt an indescribable elation. He would get his very own grad student, whatever that meant. Maybe this grad student could tell him what the thing was. Could he use the grad student to remove the crate itself?

"Can I do anything I want with the grad student?" he asked.

"Just don't break him. Oh, and don't give him notions."

"Notions?"

"It's bad when they get notions."

Wilbur wasn't sure what these "notions" were but readily agreed.

"Well, that's it then."

"But wait, how will you know where to send him?"

"The device got delivered to you, so why wouldn't a grad student?"

"*You* sent the device?"

"Of course not. There would be no point sending a grad student if I sent the device."

Wilbur muttered an apology.

"You said your wife was my friend," Greta pointed out.

"But you don't know which friend."

"Should it matter? Friends are friends. They're quite fungible, you know."

"But ..." Wilbur was uncertain how to react. What if she sent the grad student to another friend's husband? Then the grad student would answer a different question that a different guy had.

"Wait. Is she the type of friend I should ignore? Tell me now, because I'll lend the grad student to someone else."

"No, no, please don't do that. I'm sure Sarah is a good friend."

"Then what's the issue?" the professor demanded.

"You still need the address."

"Have this Sarah give it to me."

The phone clicked before he could object. Wilbur sighed and walked toward the kitchen. It would not be a fun conversation.

Chapter 6

Wilbur was right next to the door when the bell rang, and the sound startled him. There was no commotion upstairs, so Sarah must not have heard it. Or maybe she was being coy. It probably was for the best. She would have been polite to the guest, but Wilbur wanted to avoid troubling her. He had promised to deal with the mess, and this was part of dealing with it. Besides, he only had the grad student for a day and did not wish to share him.

The grad student was not what Wilbur had expected. Instead of a sharp-eyed young career woman, he was greeted with a frumpy-looking man in his thirties. Wilbur wasn't sure why he'd envisioned a sharp-eyed young career woman. Perhaps he imagined a younger version of the professor, though he'd never met her and had no idea what professors look like before they become professors.

Wilbur tried to hide his surprise. He hoped the man hadn't noticed. It would not do to alienate him right off the bat. Was this what the professor meant by 'not giving him notions'? With an awkward smile, Wilbur shook the proffered hand.

"Andrew," the man declared, wiping his galoshes on the doormat. It wasn't raining, and Wilbur was unsure why his galoshes needed wiping or why he wore galoshes at all. Maybe his job required it.

Realizing that he hadn't introduced himself, Wilbur did so and invited Andrew in.

A muffled voice came from upstairs. "Tell her I'll be down in a moment to make coffee."

"Thanks, hon," Wilbur replied. Did Sarah think the professor was coming, or had she too envisioned a sharp-eyed young career woman? Wilbur felt guilty. Maybe he should have been more specific when relaying the conversation to his wife. He had assumed she didn't want details. He hoped she wouldn't get angry and was certain she would.

"It's—" Wilbur began before turning toward the man. "Are you a graduate student?"

"I'm afraid so," he quipped, placing his hat on the rack.

"It's a grad student named Andrew," Wilbur called out.

After a long pause, a muffled "never mind" came from upstairs.

Wilbur gave the man an apologetic look. "Sorry, she must be busy."

He led the way toward the living room. "Have you ever seen her with ... " he began before stopping himself. It wasn't an appropriate question. The man wasn't here to gossip about Sarah's private life, and he'd probably report back everything they said.

"Nah, I don't get to socialize much."

Wilbur wasn't sure what to say to this. He didn't socialize much either, now that he thought about it. Did that make Wilbur a grad student? He hoped not. If it wasn't for Sarah and work, he'd barely have any human contact at all. This was an unsettling thought, the tenuous thread by which he dangled above complete isolation. If that thread broke, could he sew another in time? Two threads would be better, maybe even more. Wilbur resolved to try, though he did not know how. But before he tried anything, he had to deal with the device. Who would want to befriend a man with a device?

This made him anxious, and he suddenly was grateful for Sarah. Without her, where would he be? What was the expression: better the wrong woman than no woman. Or was it the other way? He couldn't be certain whether Sarah was the right woman or the wrong woman; he'd only had fleeting contact with others. But she certainly was *a* woman.

Rummaging in the kitchen felt disrespectful. This was Sarah's place, just as the basement was his. But Wilbur had to offer Andrew *something*. Especially since he voluntarily had come to help. This gave Wilbur pause. It was voluntary, wasn't it? It hadn't sounded voluntary.

"Sorry to trouble you," Wilbur offered with an apologetic grin.

"No trouble," Andrew replied, casting his eyes about the room. "If I wasn't doing this, I'd be doing something else."

"How are your, er, studies going?" Wilbur inquired. That was what one asked a grad student, wasn't it? What else would a grad student have to talk about.

"They're going," he grinned.

Wilbur finally managed a pitcher of juice and a couple of cookies, but Andrew didn't seem interested. Apparently, he was on some sort of diet. This made Wilbur feel better. If the grad student was in a position to fuss over diet, surely there was nothing to worry about.

"Shall we get to it then?" Andrew asked, his voice electric with barely-suppressed excitement. Wilbur wondered what the man had been told.

Wilbur had unpacked the crate in anticipation of the visit, and the basement was cluttered. Andrew ignored the black bags lining the side tables and paid little mind to the few remaining tufts of packing material, though he heeded Wilbur's warning not to handle the stuff. It was the device and the device alone which drew his interest.

Andrew scrutinized it for some time, while Wilbur maintained a listless silence. He did not wish to disrupt the man's thoughts, thoughts which could prove singularly useful undisrupted. But the wait quickly grew intolerable. Wilbur wondered aloud how the crate got into the basement. It was an idle remark, meant to dispel the oppressive quiet. He didn't expect a response and was surprised when Andrew looked up.

"They must have assembled it from parts."

Wilbur shook his head. "Why would they bother to disassemble and then reassemble it?"

Andrew gave him an odd look. "Disassemble what?"

It took a moment for Wilbur to grasp what he meant. He suddenly felt very stupid. The idea simply hadn't occurred to him. It seemed obvious, now that someone said it.

Wilbur had assumed the device was transported in the form he found it. Any assembly would require disassembly. But there was no reason it couldn't have arrived in small manageable parts, which then were assembled in the basement. Wilbur felt desperate to prove he wasn't a fool.

"What about the crate?" he asked, realizing it was a silly question even as he spoke. He hoped Andrew would charitably misconstrue it. Didn't that happen in those radio comedies? The protagonist said something inane, which the other party reframed as clever. Wilbur didn't relish being a lucky buffoon, but it beat being an unlucky one. Would Andrew want to help a buffoon of any sort?

The grad student glanced at the locks and hinges. "Why couldn't the crate also have been assembled?"

Wilbur's face fell. Unlucky buffoon it was. But Andrew spared him.

"I see what you mean, though. Why bother assembling a crate? That's what you're talking about, right?" Was he just being kind, or did he actually agree? Wilbur felt particularly inadequate. What type of buffoon couldn't even *tell* if he was lucky?

Wilbur clasped the lifeline and gave a sage nod. "Exactly. Why bother building the crate? Wouldn't there be a bunch of small empty boxes instead?"

"That makes sense. Unless the crate is necessary for protection, or maybe security." Before Wilbur could reply, Andrew proceeded to refute himself. "But why bother with the packing material in that case? If it arrived in smaller boxes, they'd discard the stuff."

"Maybe it's expensive?" Wilbur ventured, unsure why he was trying to debunk his own theory.

"Then they'd keep it themselves. Why would they fill the crate with it? Maybe it was intended to be reshipped."

"How could it be shipped from down here?"

"Exactly," Andrew exclaimed, much to Wilbur's delight. "The packing material makes no sense. If it was a prank, I could see it. But this hardly strikes me as a prank." He looked around again, then assumed an air of decision. "I agree — it must have been delivered like this."

Wilbur wasn't sure why the grad student was impressed by this argument more than any other, but it didn't matter. The original conundrum remained: how did it get in?

"But what if it *was* in parts?" Andrew continued.

The readjudication of this issue didn't bother Wilbur. He already had been absolved of stupidity. Andrew could rehash and reexamine and reconsider as much as he liked now. Perhaps it was a good thing. Wilbur decided to follow his lead.

"How much would the lightest part weigh?" he asked.

"I'm not sure. I'm not even sure what this thing is. What do you know about it?"

Wilbur was pondering the weight and did not notice the question.

Andrew sighed. "The professor mentioned a manual of some sort?"

"Oh right," Wilbur stammered, struggling to remember where he had placed the thing. He gave an awkward smile. "Sorry. I'll go find it."

Wilbur searched his pockets, then looked behind the black bags. He hoped it wasn't under one of those. Then he remembered. It was in his bedroom nightstand, where he kept it every night. There was a certain comfort sleeping next to it, knowing it was there and nowhere else. The manual made the device less mysterious, less dangerous. Even if he did not understand the words.

"Thank you," Andrew replied when handed the booklet, before immersing himself in it. The words had a slightly sarcastic edge.

Wilbur murmured another apology, but the student was oblivious to anything other than the manual. Wilbur sat on the stairs and studied the bags of packing material, trying not to grow impatient. At length, Andrew closed the book and motioned him over. Only a few minutes had passed, but it felt a lot longer.

"I'll need to study this in detail to be sure," he explained, "but I think I understand the essentials. It's clear that the device has a yield of 1.72 megatons, though I'm not sure whether that is optimal or expected."

Wilbur gave an audible gasp. He had read the manual, and this had *not* been clear to him. Nothing had.

"1.72 megatons sounds like a lot," he whispered once the initial shock had passed.

Andrew nodded, then thought for a few moments.

"I don't think they would risk assembling the core on-site, so let's look at that. A purely fissile weapon typically would have a yield of a kiloton per kilogram. For 1.72 megatons that would be" — he calculated in his head — "a sphere of uranium around sixty centimeters in diameter and weighing two tons."

This sounded plausible to Wilbur and would explain much about the crate.

"But that just would be the uranium," Andrew continued. "I'd guess the other components of the core would be at least three to five times bigger and weigh as much."

"But they could assemble that bit, right?"

Andrew shook his head. "It would be too difficult to assemble here. Aside from the obvious danger, there are extremely precise tolerances involved. The core would have to come as a unit."

Something about this new estimate didn't sit right with Wilbur. He glanced at the device. "How wide did you say it would have to be?"

"At least two meters. So, um, six feet or so." Andrew smiled and gestured at the weapon. "Yeah, it's obviously nowhere near that size."

"The width of the fat part is three feet. I measured it," Wilbur announced with more than a little pride. It seemed an odd thing to be proud of. He wondered whether other people were proud of such things. Shouldn't a man have more to be proud of? He was tempted to ask Andrew, but decided it would be impolite. What could a grad student be proud of?

Andrew nodded. "The core can't be more than a foot and a half of that. Maybe two." He looked at Wilbur. "There's probably a lot of stuff in there besides the core, you know."

Those words annoyed Wilbur. No, he did not know. If he knew, he wouldn't require Andrew's expertise. He wasn't sure he cared exactly what "stuff" was in there. All he needed to know was what the thing did and maybe how to use it. Maybe. He wondered if that would be wise. Not knowing probably would be for the best.

"Six kilotons per kilogram."

Wilbur looked at Andrew, who now had a self-assured air.

"Six kilotons per kilogram," he repeated. "In principle, it is possible to achieve that. Though ... it may not be a Teller-Ulam configuration."

"Tell her what?"

"The yield of an atomic bomb comes entirely from the fission of uranium 235 or plutonium 239, so you probably think the much higher yield of a thermonuclear bomb comes entirely from fusion. Basically, a bunch of tritium detonated by a tiny atomic bomb." He looked at Wilbur. "That's what I used to think."

"I really know nothing about it at all," Wilbur confessed. He hoped this wasn't a faux pas. Was it rude to say something like that? Knowing *nothing* seemed dismissive. One knew nothing about subjects which deserved obscurity. How would this reflect on those who knew something?

"Nothing?" Andrew asked. He seemed surprised rather than offended.

Wilbur took the opportunity to correct the misstep. "Well, almost nothing." Almost nothing was better than nothing, less than judgmental and not quite a lie. Besides, who truly knew nothing about a subject? Almost nothing implied difficulty rather than irrelevance. It made the man who knew something a scholar, an intellectual, a person of attainment. Not some squirrelly eccentric muttering to himself in the park.

And it wasn't entirely untrue. Wilbur had been taught a little about nuclear bombs. He was supposed to hide under a school desk when the siren went off. But this was not very helpful at the moment. He didn't even own a school desk.

Andrew gently explained. "Fusion bombs originally used a small plutonium plug surrounded by tritium, but that wasn't ideal. Tritium needs to stay cold, and it decays quickly. Higher yields can be achieved by triggering a secondary fission reaction. Uranium 238 can't sustain a chain reaction under ordinary conditions, but it can, briefly, under the extreme conditions of a fusion explosion. Modern devices use lithium deuteride for fusion and pack a U-238 secondary around this. About half the yield of the bomb comes from the unenriched uranium."

"I thought the core was just uranium."

Andrew's eyebrow furrowed, but his voice held no reproach. "I said I was calculating with purely fissile material, and I also said there was other stuff. The heaviest part is the uranium and plutonium, of course. Around nineteen grams per cubic centimeter. Even steel's only seven. The core also contains shaped chemical explosives, stuffing, and shielding, though these probably don't take much space. I imagine it's mostly filled with lithium deuteride. This is very light, but a lot is needed. All told, I think my estimate of three to five times the purely fissile size is about right."

"But you said that would be bigger than three feet."

"At one kiloton per kilogram, it would be. At six, the purely fissile diameter would be thirty centimeters. If the remainder takes three times the space, we get a forty-four centimeter diameter, or seventeen inches. At five times, we get twenty inches. Even that would be under two feet in diameter. Mind you, the actual uranium ball only would be ten inches in diameter, since it produces just half the yield. Most of the rest would be the lithium deuteride. I just used the purely fissile diameter to get the ballpark size. It's a useful rule of thumb."

"Have you built one?" Wilbur asked in astonishment. Was this something every grad student learned? He imagined a class on bomb-making and wondered what sort of exam it had.

"Oh no," Andrew laughed. "That would be illegal."

This raised an important question, something Wilbur had been fuzzy on from the start. "Is it illegal for me to have it?" he asked.

Andrew thought for a few seconds. "I'm not sure. It depends how it's classified. Weapon laws vary by state. Some places ban sales, others ban possession. It's quite possible that you're allowed to own but not buy it. Or, more precisely, nobody is allowed to sell it to you. If that's the case, you're probably fine."

"Is that the case? Am I fine?" Even if the law said so, Wilbur wasn't sure how he could be fine with a nuclear bomb in his basement.

Andrew shrugged. "I'm not sure." He gave a grin. "But I *am* pretty sure you're not allowed to use it. That's probably true in every state."

This hardly clarified anything for Wilbur, but he felt better. If the law wasn't obvious to an expert, how could a lay person be expected to know such things? Was Andrew an expert? He decided to ask.

"I wouldn't say I'm an expert," Andrew replied with an expression of distaste. "That is such a fraught word."

"But it sounds like you know quite a lot about these things."

"It's just an" — he hesitated for a moment — "interest of mine."

"Do you know how to build one?"

"I have a general picture of how it's done." Andrew caressed the device with his eyes, then pressed his cheek against it. "But I never thought I would get to see one, especially this close."

Wilbur cringed. "Please be careful. What if it's … sensitive?"

"I wouldn't worry," Andrew promised. "We're safe. Well, as safe as can be while standing next to a nuclear bomb. Even the older devices wouldn't go off easily. Do you know how hard it is to get one of these things to work?"

Wilbur wasn't sure what Andrew meant by "older" devices. Had they been around long enough to make such distinctions? It felt like these things were pretty recent. He couldn't remember a time without them, but that hardly was surprising. There were many things he couldn't remember, and it didn't mean they hadn't happened. He realized

Andrew was waiting for an answer. Apparently the question wasn't rhetorical. Wilbur confessed he did not, in fact, know this.

Andrew gave a light laugh. "Well, I can see why you're concerned. The thing certainly looks scary." He puffed his mouth and gestured an explosion with his hands. "But it's not a big landmine waiting to be set off by a feather." He smiled. "Believe it or not, the army is pretty adamant about not getting blown up by their own bombs. Have you ever heard of one going off?"

Wilbur shook his head. Of course, that didn't mean one *hadn't* gone off. He doubted he would hear it from far away. There were no wars nearby, or none that he knew of. He was fairly certain the newspaper would have said if a war was nearby. It probably would be deemed newsworthy.

"There's a reason they're so hard to produce," Andrew continued. "It's difficult to get the configuration just right. You need to know the equation of state, and nobody knows the equation of state." He placed his palm against the device and smiled. "Nobody but a few government scientists."

"Do you know it?" Wilbur asked.

"Of course not," Andrew chuckled. "And I wouldn't be allowed to talk about it even if I did." He grew pensive for a moment, then returned his attention to Wilbur. "The point is you could drop this out of an airplane and it wouldn't go off. Not unless properly triggered. The biggest danger to us right now is radiation."

Wilbur recoiled.

Andrew produced a small glass vial filled with

gel. "I checked that when I arrived. Radiation causes bubbles." He shook the vial. "No bubbles, no radiation. But you almost always get a few from stray gamma rays. It's astonishing how little radiation there is down here. There hasn't been a single bubble this whole time. I'm sure you'll be happy to know you have no radon in your basement."

Wilbur never had considered that possibility. Radon could be a problem in a cramped space like this. Had it been killing him slowly this whole time? Wilbur wasn't sure how much faith to place in an ampule of gel.

"You're a lot more likely to die from that than this," Andrew promised, playfully slapping the side of the device. Wilbur winced, closing his eyes as the hollow ring reverberated.

"Relax," Andrew laughed. "This bomb is very well-shielded. And apparently so is this basement. You probably get less radiation down here than in your bedroom."

"Should I sleep here, instead?" Wilbur asked.

"Not if you want to stay married."

Andrew assumed a pensive expression. "What puzzles me is the absence of a trigger."

"Trigger?"

"Something to control it. I don't see any controls on the outside. It wouldn't be great if somebody else had the trigger."

He allowed this to sink in.

"You think somebody else has it?" Wilbur asked after a few seconds.

Andrew shrugged, clearly surprised by Wilbur's

lack of concern. "I doubt it."

"I see what you mean, though. Without the trigger, I'm just storing somebody else's stuff." It didn't feel that way, though. Ever since Wilbur's conversation with Erik, the device felt like it was his. He had grown decidedly more apathetic about its removal and prayed Sarah wouldn't notice. The thing still had to go, but failure did not bother him as much anymore.

"Personally, I'd be less comfortable with a nuclear bomb in my basement if somebody else had the trigger," Andrew remarked.

Wilbur looked at him and realized what the man was getting at. He eyed the stairs. Would it be rude to abandon Andrew down there? He *had* offered him juice and cookies. Surely, that satisfied the demands of etiquette. How far would he have to run before he was free and clear? Not just of it, but everything. How far could a man run? No, not a man. Him. How far could *he* run before his legs failed and he returned hat in hand. Or lost the means to find his way back or forward or anywhere else.

Wilbur suddenly felt silly. He headed for the stairs, quick but now calm. There was no need to flee, at least at the moment. A minute later he returned, more than a little out of breath. In his hand was the small box with the red button.

⁓❀⁓

"That's it!" Andrew clapped his hands together in delight, then gave Wilbur a slightly reproachful glance. "You should have mentioned this."

"It won't open," Wilbur observed, as if sufficient explanation.

Andrew didn't seem bothered. "Hmmm ... let's try this."

He walked over to the small grey window on the side of the device, raised his own hand, then reconsidered. Instead, he gently guided Wilbur's thumb over and pressed it against the window. The button case popped open and glowed. Andrew carefully closed the case.

"Ok, let's try again." He pressed his own thumb against the window. Nothing happened.

"As I thought. It is tuned to your thumbprint."

Wilbur turned red. "Why didn't *you* do it?"

"Since it is in your basement, I thought you should have control of it."

This made sense, but Wilbur couldn't shake his irritation.

"It probably wouldn't have worked anyway," Andrew added. "I suspect it already was tuned to you."

"Because it is in my basement?"

"Because you may have touched it already."

"But it never popped open before," Wilbur protested.

"That's probably because you didn't hold it long enough." Andrew thought for a second. "Or maybe because the trigger was upstairs."

"How do you know?" The man's knowledge of the topic seemed oddly specific, and Wilbur couldn't help but feel he was hiding something. Had *he* sent it? It was paranoid to even think such a thing, and Wilbur suddenly felt ashamed. The poor fellow was trying to help, that was all. Besides, Andrew's involvement was entirely serendipitous. He'd had no say in it. This made Wilbur feel even worse. The man really did have no say. He resolved to be nicer and hoped his question hadn't sounded critical.

Andrew shrugged. "It's a common mechanism for computer security."

"You could have warned me."

"What would be the fun in that?" Andrew chuckled. Then he grew serious. "Besides, if it was meant for you, it makes sense for you to have control of it."

"Nobody should have control of it," Wilbur declared with more warmth than he felt. Maybe Andrew should have control of the device. A man should have control of something.

"It wasn't delivered to 'nobody'," Andrew pointed out. "It was delivered to you."

"Misdelivered," Wilbur corrected.

"If you say so." Before Wilbur could object, Andrew smiled at him. "Well, there's nothing to worry about. It's in your capable hands. Just don't press the button and everything will be fine."

"What does the button do?"

"What do you think it does?"

Wilbur pondered this for a moment. "I'm not sure I want to know."

"Then don't press it. That way you won't find out. It's never good to press a big red button, unless you want to press a big red button."

"Still," — Andrew's eyes caressed the device — "it seems small."

"Not to me."

Andrew clearly hadn't been expecting a reply. He

looked at Wilbur for a moment, then grinned. "1.72 megatons is a lot for something this size."

"I thought it fit your calculations." Had the man made a mistake? Maybe fallibility was what distinguished graduate students from professors.

Andrew frowned. "That assumed an extraordinarily high yield density. In theory it could be attained, but I'm not aware of any real device with such an efficient design. On the other hand, I doubt the manual is lying."

"Why not?" Wilbur wondered aloud.

"Why would it?"

He had a point. Wilbur could see no reason someone would go to such lengths to build and transport the device, only to lie about such a detail.

"On the other hand," Andrew continued, "we don't know where it came from. Maybe it's not one of ours." There always seemed to be an "other hand" but rarely a first one. Wilbur wondered what had become of it. Maybe it was vestigial.

"Not one of ours?" he echoed, barely registering the words. Did Andrew have others? That could explain his uncanny knowledge of the subject. Maybe he was a collector. Wilbur considered offering it to him. Surely, a collector would be willing to collect it.

"As in not made domestically. It's a disturbing thought," Andrew considered.

Wilbur had to agree. What else did the enemy have which nobody knew about? Maybe this was their plan: to deliver nuclear bombs to basements throughout the land. Wilbur imagined the enemy would want to keep the control buttons in that case. But would they really? Giving random people control could achieve the same end as war, but without incurring any blame. Who could fault the enemy for misdelivering nuclear weapons? If anything, they lost valuable — what did the military types call it — ordinance. That was the word. Just like a town bylaw, but less worrisome.

Andrew looked at him. "I know what you're getting at, though."

Wilbur had no idea what Andrew meant by this. What was Wilbur getting at? It bothered him that he did not know. Shouldn't a man know what he was getting at? He hoped Andrew would tell him. It seemed at least as important as knowing about the device.

"But where could it be from?"

Andrew shrugged. "Who can tell. I'm sure only a few countries can produce something like this."

For a while the man was quiet, and Wilbur assumed he was considering the matter.

"It still bothers me, though," he finally announced.

"The country of origin?"

"I don't think the stairs would have held it," Andrew continued. "But they could have propped up the stairs. Movers sometimes do."

It took a few moments for Wilbur to realize what he was talking about. Why had he come back to this? They already had failed to explain it and moved on. Maybe there was a reason Andrew was returning to this particular line of inquiry. Was it the key to getting rid of the thing? That would make sense. Knowing how to get something into a place and out of a place were two sides of the same coin.

"It's unlikely," he pointed out. "They only were here a short time, I think. Besides, wouldn't that make a lot of noise? My wife would have noticed a lot of noise."

"I see," Andrew replied. "So there wasn't much noise? I can't see how they got it in here without making noise. Even if they disassembled and reassembled it."

Wilbur was puzzled. Hadn't they already ruled out that scenario? Surely, once something was discarded it was gone for good. Could ideas be brought back? It made him wonder what else could be brought back. If he managed to get rid of the device, would it come back?

He noticed Andrew's eyes on his own. The man had an odd expression. Did he think Wilbur was lying?

"How do you know the device was delivered?" Andrew asked after an uncomfortably long silence.

"Well, Sarah ... my wife told me."

"What exactly did she say?"

It seemed an intrusive question. Why did it matter what words she had used? He tried to recall. "There was a package ... "

"But not what the package was? Did you ask?"

Wilbur felt his temper rising. Of course he had asked! But how could he explain this without maligning Sarah to her friend's grad student?

"She was busy with other things and didn't see."

Andrew gave him a cryptic glance but appeared to accept the answer.

"So you don't know that this was the package she

referred to."

"What else could it be?" Wilbur replied with some heat.

"No need to get upset. I'm just trying to get to the bottom of this. You did ask for my help."

"Well, for the professor's," Wilbur replied before realizing how rude it was. The student's crestfallen expression echoed this.

"I'm sorry," Wilbur hastened to add. "I'm grateful for your help, and you know a lot more than the professor."

Andrew looked horrified. "Don't ever say that," he whispered. "Please."

Wilbur was unsure what to say and simply promised not to.

The student exhaled in relief and took a moment to recompose himself. With a smile and clap of the hands, he turned to Wilbur.

"Well, let's get back to the nuclear bomb."

"My point is that we should be careful what we infer," Andrew explained.

"Infer?"

"Let's determine precisely what we know and figure out the most probable answer." The man clearly was in his element now.

Wilbur gave a nervous nod and hoped he wouldn't be called upon to do any of the "figuring out." All this scientific stuff was best left to scientists.

"We know the device is here," Andrew began. "And we know you had a delivery that day. Neither you nor your wife saw the delivery, and there is no manifest. So we do not know that this was the delivery."

"Now wait a—"

"When did you last enter the basement?"

"Yesterday."

Andrew shook his head. "Before you found the device. How long had it been?"

Wilbur looked at the ceiling and tried to remember. "I'm not sure. A while."

"A week, a month, a year?"

Had it been a year? More than a month, probably. It was so hard to recall that sort of detail. Wilbur felt a growing disquiet. Maybe something unpleasant had happened in the basement. What could have been unpleasant enough to blot out his memory? Clearly not this. He had no trouble remembering this. Months. It had been at least two months. What was the point of having a basement workshop if he never visited it? Months seemed too long. He noticed Andrew's eyes on him.

"I'm really not sure. Maybe a month or two."

"So it's fair to say that you aren't down here very often."

It didn't sound fair, but it did sound accurate. "The air is musty, and I've been very busy," Wilbur protested. "Normally, I do a lot more down here."

"But not then," Andrew insisted, oblivious to the rest. This sounded vaguely judgmental. Was he being judged by a grad student? It felt demeaning. Wilbur wondered why he cared what a grad student thought of him.

"Probably not," he replied.

"So the crate could have been down here for longer. It need not have been delivered that day."

Wilbur always had connected the crate with the delivery Sarah mentioned. He had looked, and there were no other packages at the time. But it was an intriguing idea.

"Even so, there's the same problem," he pointed out. "How did it get in here?"

Andrew shrugged. "I don't know, but let's see where this takes us. You simply assumed it was delivered that day."

Despite the man's dispassionate tone, something about the way he spoke grated on Wilbur.

"It was the obvious thing to assume. I'm sure you would have done the same."

"Be that as it may, don't you find it odd that nobody came looking for it? I'd come looking for it were it mine. Wouldn't you?"

Wilbur was about to object to Andrew's tone but stopped himself. The man was here to help, and it wouldn't do to quibble over his manner of speech or take umbrage at every question. Besides, this did strike Wilbur as odd.

"It *is* an expensive mistake to ignore," he agreed. Suddenly, he had an idea. "Maybe they came, but nobody was home."

"I imagine they would keep trying," Andrew replied.

That made sense. Besides, when was Sarah not home?

"I don't think it was delivered." Andrew declared, his voice now decisive.

"Then what was?"

"Who knows. Maybe some small package that got lost in the commotion. Or maybe the deliverymen didn't deliver anything. Would you have noticed if they took something instead?"

The thought disturbed Wilbur. Maybe Sarah's negligence had led to theft. Or worse. Who knew what nasty surprise they had hidden somewhere in the house. Could it be worse than a nuclear bomb?

"That still doesn't explain how it got here," Wilbur complained. "If anything, you've made the problem worse."

"I haven't made it anything. It is what it is. We're just no longer constrained by flawed assumptions."

Wilbur didn't consider his assumptions flawed. How would anyone have reacted under the circumstances? Despite this, it wasn't irritation or embarrassment that he felt. Just curiosity with a tinge of hope. It sounded like this grad student actually knew how to find the answer. Wilbur made a mental note to thank the professor. And Erik. He mustn't forget Erik.

"So what do you think happened?" he asked the man, now with a hint of deference.

Andrew shook his head. "I'm not sure. I have some theories, none of them good."

Wilbur sucked in his breath. "You think we're in danger?"

"You mean aside from standing next to a nuclear bomb of unknown provenance?" Andrew laughed. He rapped the metal casing with his knuckle, and Wilbur cringed again. Was he doing that on purpose?

"I mean that the theories lack evidence," he explained. "They're not worth sharing at this point."

Seeing the disappointment on Wilbur's face, he gave a sigh.

"Well if I were to speculate, I'd say it has been in the basement all along. I think you just first noticed it that day."

"But how—"

"It's amazing what the mind can fail to notice when distracted."

Wilbur wondered whether the man spoke from experience. Was this how a grad student survived? Not noticing sounded like a handy tool.

"Or perhaps you simply discounted it as impossible," Andrew continued. "You probably avoided the space it occupies without knowing why. Was anything there before the crate?"

Wilbur thought for a moment. "I used to have a big table down here, but it was filthy and couldn't be used for anything."

"What happened to it?"

"I think I took it apart and threw out the wood. Or maybe I donated it. It was a while ago."

"How long ago?"

Wilbur racked his brain. "I really don't recall." He leaned toward Andrew. "Do you think that's odd?"

The man shrugged. "Maybe. Or maybe it's just as you said. I have no idea."

"Is there any way to find out?"

Andrew pondered this in silence. Wilbur felt a rush of gratitude. Despite being busy with countless other things, the man was going to such lengths to help him.

"It's beyond my expertise," Andrew finally

acceded.

Wilbur's stomach sank. "What should I do?"

"I think the first step would be to determine exactly what type of bomb it is. Maybe we can deduce its origin that way. Everything else may follow from that."

Wilbur wanted to shout that determining this exact thing was why he had asked Andrew for help in the first place. Or, more precisely, been granted his help by another.

"But how? I thought you were supposed to know." It sounded plaintive, but Andrew didn't seem to notice. He appeared to be debating something in his head.

After a few moments, he reached a decision.

"I know a professor who can help. He's retired now, but used to be a nuclear physicist at a national lab. I think he can tell you what it is."

Wilbur felt relief wash over him. This professor sounded like just the man for the job. He would know what it was. More importantly, he would know what to do. If need be, the FBI would listen to a genuine nuclear physicist. Maybe this professor would become enamored of the device and take it with him. Surely, such a man would know how to remove it.

This last thought bothered Wilbur. If the thing was intended for him, it felt wrong to give it away. And what would Andrew think? After all the man had done, it seemed ungrateful to bestow it on another. Worse, to someone Andrew had introduced him to. The whole thing made Wilbur feel dirty. It was too much drama, and he did not like drama.

Maybe he should let Sarah deal with that side of things. He made a note to gently sound her on this.

"Would you like me to do so?" Andrew asked.

"Please!" Wilbur replied, clasping the man's hand. "And thank you."

Andrew extracted his hand with an uneasy smile. "Ok, I'll go make the phone call. Nice meeting you."

He bolted up the stairs, but Wilbur didn't mind. Hope had been restored.

After the first day without word from anyone, this hope began to wane. By the end of the second, Wilbur had decided it was another dead end. The world was made of dead ends these days. He wondered if there was any other kind.

Chapter 7

A shoulder squeeze from Erik was the first sign of something amiss. Was it supposed to be a sympathetic squeeze? It felt a bit too strong and lingered a bit too long. Erik's expression seemed apologetic, with a hint of something else. Maybe he was sorry for squeezing too hard, or at all. Such things could be misconstrued, and who knew where a misconstrued squeeze could lead.

Wilbur wished he was better at reading expressions. Maybe he and Sarah... He stopped himself. Such speculation was pointless. It would change nothing. Before Wilbur could say anything, their manager waved Erik over.

A visit was not remarkable in itself. Wilbur had plenty of visits in the course of a typical day, often from Erik. But not like this. The man was not the touchy-feely sort, and the gesture was wildly out of character. Over the next hour, the shoulder squeeze came to occupy a larger and larger share of Wilbur's thoughts. He could not pinpoint precisely what disturbed him about it. Maybe it wasn't the squeeze at all, but what it portended. If it was sympathetic, then something required sympathy. How bad did that something have to be to draw sympathy from a man like Erik?

Wilbur's mind raced. What could be wrong? There was one obvious candidate, two if he counted the job. Was that what this was about? Maybe Erik had been promoted over him. Maybe Erik had been *retained* over him. Were there layoffs? That was the last thing he needed right now, amidst the bills and chaos and Sarah's mounting displeasure. Wilbur imagined himself unemployed and home with her all day, every day. Which of them would fail first?

There was another scenario. It too involved Sarah, though in a different capacity. He felt sick at the thought. Wouldn't a policeman have broken the news? Why would Erik know first? Unless he'd been responsible. Maybe Erik ploughed into her on the highway. Or maybe he just ploughed her.

Wilbur couldn't imagine Sarah and Erik doing such a thing, but wasn't that always what the husband said? It was the oldest story in the world. Unhappy wife, best friend. It was bad to have one, worse to have both. Such affairs never ended well, except maybe for them. He brushed aside the thought. It was unthinkable, and he had no room for unthinkable thoughts.

Predictably, it wasn't long before they were all he had room for. The device and everything else were banished from his mind. How could he find out for sure? Wilbur felt a peculiar embarrassment. It was shameful to be deceived, even if it wasn't his fault. Nobody respected *that* husband. It meant he had chosen poorly or driven his wife into another man's arms. What good could be said of such a husband? Wilbur desperately wished not to be that man, to laugh away the silly notion. But his suspicion would not be gainsaid. Though entirely unsure what to say or what he hoped to learn, he dialed home. Sarah didn't pick up until the eighth ring.

"What is it now?" she barked into the phone.

Wilbur was taken aback by her brusqueness, though relieved that it was not specifically intended for him. She had no idea who was calling. This was bad in its own way, however. Was she already on guard about something, or did she always answer like this? It hardly seemed an appropriate way to greet callers. Maybe her home life was a nightmarish stream of telemarketers. Wilbur had read of such a thing. There even was a name for the syndrome, but he could not recall it.

What about her friends? Surely she did not answer *their* calls this way. But how would she know? Maybe they understood her predicament and made allowances. He wondered why he hadn't noticed before. Did he ever call her during the day? It seemed like the sort of thing he must have done. That didn't excuse her manners though. It was bad phone etiquette at the very least. What if he had been somebody important?

"I just thought I'd call and see how you are," Wilbur replied, voice wavering. It made him sound guilty. Wasn't that what an unfaithful husband did: call home and check on the wife to assuage his own guilt. Was he guilty of thinking her guilty? He expected a sharp reply, something like "why are you suddenly so worried?" Sarah had a special way of putting him on the spot, finding ulterior motives for innocent words. Wilbur preferred a tirade, and a tirade was what he got. Just not the one he expected.

"It's about time you called back. I guess I'm less important than whatever stupid thing you're working on." Sarah truly was livid. It was the only time she resorted to direct insults rather than her usual refined cruelties.

Wilbur knew he had his work cut out. Learning what had angered her would be a long and painful process, and he could kiss a tranquil evening goodbye. With a sigh, he considered how to begin.

Sarah did so for him, unprompted.

"I guess that idiot friend of yours finally told you. I called five times."

"But, I didn't ..." Wilbur began to explain, now completely at a loss. Had the operator somehow directed her to Erik? Wilbur had been at his desk most of the day, and Sarah had his extension. Her calls should have gone through, but mentioning this would not help.

"I'm sorry," he offered.

The simple sincerity of this appeared to catch his wife off guard, and there was an uncomfortable silence. It puzzled Wilbur. Why was this time different? He had apologized to her on countless occasions. Sometimes it felt like all he ever did. He wondered whether this was her food, her sustenance. Why else would she be with a guy who always had to apologize. Or a guy who would.

She finally replied, slightly less snippy.

"You're going to be. You get home right now."

"But I've got a meeting at four," he protested before realizing it didn't matter. Sarah needed to know he was there for her, that she was the most important thing to him. Was it all a game to cover up the calls to Erik and heaven knew what else? Maybe she and Erik had been conspiring about the device too.

This was the first time Wilbur had thought about the device since the shoulder squeeze. Whatever problems he now faced were in addition to the device, not in lieu of it. This weighed heavily on his morale. It was hard to see the point of climbing out of a little pit at the bottom of a much larger one.

"I'll be right home," Wilbur quickly amended.

"See that you are."

"But what is this about?" he asked. The line was dead.

Even from a distance, Wilbur could hear the strange noise. For a moment he worried the device had been activated, but the sound wasn't industrial or ominous, just an indecipherable murmur. He doubted the device made any noise, much less this noise. It was a one-shot deal. He wondered if the thing included a warning siren or countdown.

The murmur grew in volume as Wilbur neared home, and he began to make out indistinct voices. The din clearly came from the vicinity of his house. That spawned a new worry. Had Sarah done something crazy? She didn't sound like her usual self on the phone. The car accelerated. Was she ok? Wilbur felt a rising panic. Maybe it was an aneurysm. He had read that certain temperaments were at greater risk. He careened around the corner, dreading to see an ambulance or police car.

Wilbur slammed on the brakes and narrowly avoided hitting a young man. A chaos of people surrounded his house, sprawling into the street. He stared in confusion. There were no flashing lights, and the crowd was too large to be gawkers. Besides, it normally was a quiet block. He doubted that this many people passed by in a whole week.

The voices were not hysterical or discordant. There was a certain rhythm to them, almost a unity. He surveyed the scene from the car. It was a bunch of kids, though he couldn't tell how young. They seemed rather self-assured for high-school kids, and he decided they must be in college. Some of the kids were holding signs and others were screaming at or about something.

The crowd was facing away from Wilbur and must not have heard the car approach. He was unnerved by the near miss, but nobody else seemed to notice. The kid he almost struck turned, looked him over, and returned to chanting.

There was no chance of driving through the crowd, so he got out of the car. Now he could see everything. The driveway was packed with reporters, and several news vans cluttered the street. What were they filming? Had something happened? His stomach sank. Maybe it *was* Sarah. Maybe he had missed the ambulance. But why would reporters stick around once the story left?

What if this was about the device? Wilbur felt new hope. Maybe it was like in the movies: some tenacious journalist heard of it from a colleague, connected the dots, and realized Wilbur was telling the truth. They finally would get their Pulitzer, and he'd be rid of the thing.

That didn't explain the kids, though. Maybe they were there for some other reason. If the device had become public knowledge, outside interest would be high. They probably were from one of those peace or environmental groups. Well, it was none of his concern. When the device was removed, the protesters would follow.

He picked his way through the crowd, issuing a steady stream of apologies and pardon-me's. Though jostled a bit along the way, Wilbur reached the house without trouble. In fact, nobody paid him much mind at all. He wasn't surprised by this. Wilbur was much older than the kids and was wearing a suit. They probably took him for a reporter, though most of those were younger and female. They were better groomed as well. Maybe they were television reporters and needed to manage a pleasant appearance. Could he pass for a newspaper reporter instead? Those probably weren't telegenic. A couple of the journalists shot him dirty looks as he passed. Did they think he was trying to cut in front?

The moment Wilbur produced a key, everything changed. All eyes were on him. The journalists seemed uncertain, but the crowd was not. The kids surged forward en masse while shouting, and a mob of cameramen followed. Wilbur was fumbling with the lock when he heard the commotion. He turned to see what was happening.

The kids had strangely-painted faces, many with some sort of symbol drawn on them. They carried posters and signs, and some were waving flags. These were fancifully colored and bore various acronyms and slogans, though he could made little sense of them. The chant was equally indecipherable except when it occasionally broke into boos and shouts.

Wilbur soon noticed that the crowd's vocalizations followed a certain pattern. There was a period of unintelligible clamor, some chanting, a few individual shouts, with cheers or jeers in response, and then the whole thing repeated itself.

He wondered what they were yelling about. Was his zipper down or his tie wrong? He managed a brief downward glance and exhaled in relief; the tie was red, not blue. Too shy to check his zipper, Wilbur instinctively smoothed his hair instead. This elicited a fresh round of booing, after which the crowd returned to its former cycle. He could make out some of what was said during the individual outbursts.

"Look how vain he is," someone shouted.

"Thinks a suit makes him proper," another called out.

"We know what you are," yet another chimed in.

Soon everyone was jeering.

Wilbur by now had his back firmly planted against the door, and Sarah almost knocked him over when she emerged. If he fell off the stoop, would they tear him to pieces? She looked around but did not seem surprised. Wilbur realized she must have been listening to the ruckus for some time, perhaps all day. How long *had* the crowd been there? More important, why hadn't she confronted them? Or called the police.

He looked at his wife and was taken aback by the expression on her face. The stern command, the assured impatience which dwelt in those eyes had been replaced with uncertainty, with weakness. It was unlike her, but they'd never dealt with something like this before.

Wilbur experienced a pang of irritation toward Sarah. Where was her tempestuous personality when they needed it? He felt ashamed. His wife was by his side despite what fear she harbored. She could have stayed inside.

"Look at her," one of the women in the crowd spat with disdain, and a fresh round of jeers followed, now directed at the new object of their ire. Was this about her? Wilbur couldn't imagine why they would be upset with Sarah. The device was his, even if it really wasn't.

"Enabler."

"Gender-Traitor."

"Bitch."

Wilbur felt his temper rise and instinctively stepped in front of Sarah. In so doing, he inadvertently bumped her toward the door. She didn't seem to notice. In fact, she was in a daze.

"Look at him," one of the crowd shouted. "He hit her."

"She's a victim."

"Brainwashed."

"Stupid cow."

Without thinking, Wilbur shouted at the crowd. "Leave my wife out of this."

"*His* wife."

"Possessive."

"Controlling."

"Abuser."

"What a piece of work."

One of the younger women crept forward and motioned with her hand for Sarah to join them.

"Help us help you," she coaxed.

Sarah looked around, no longer dazed. "Get out of my garden," she stammered. She almost never stammered. With most people such a thing meant uncertainty. With Sarah it did not. It seemed she would find her voice after all. Wilbur braced for the tongue-lashing, hoping she would expend herself on the crowd, knowing she would not.

The young woman retreated, shaking her head. "She's too far gone."

"Poor thing."

"What a bastard."

With this, the chanting rose to a crescendo. Wilbur searched the crowd for a sympathetic face. All he saw were angry young people and a few smirking reporters. Then he spotted a man who was neither. He clearly was a reporter of some sort but did not seem pleased like the others. He even was shaking his head in disapproval.

Before Wilbur could give it any thought, their eyes met. The man mimed the act of writing. Wilbur wasn't entirely sure what he wanted, but it looked like an invitation. Oddly enough, the other reporters kept their distance. After the initial rush they had arranged themselves in a ring but seemed hesitant to get too close. Were they afraid of the mob or of him?

Wilbur felt something wet on his shoulder. Turning, he saw tears in his wife's eyes. Was she really this weak? He felt an odd mix of pity and contempt but had little time to process it. There had been a palpable change in the crowd, a growing ugliness. He ushered Sarah inside, signaling the man to follow.

This had a surprising effect on the crowd, which let the reporter through and then grew calm. The chanting continued, but without its former virulence. Was this what they wanted all along? It struck Wilbur as an odd thing to riot over. And a pointless one. He had been trying to get a reporter's attention for weeks.

Wilbur decided the journalist had a trustworthy face. He was glad the man interviewing him had a trustworthy face. He just as easily could not have, and Wilbur couldn't afford to be picky. If he was the one who recognized the importance of the story, Wilbur wouldn't quibble over whether the man's face was trustworthy or not. He was glad it was.

The man didn't state his name, and Wilbur thought it impolite to ask. He probably was somebody famous, somebody from TV or radio or the newspaper, somebody Wilbur should recognize. Wilbur didn't want the first words out of his mouth to be a faux pas. In fact, he was unsure what to say while the man fastidiously arranged a pen and pad and recording device on the coffee table. It felt awkward to say nothing. But what if he said the wrong thing. Better nothing than the wrong something. Should he offer him something instead? It seemed the sort of thing Sarah would do.

Where was Sarah anyway? His wife had

vanished altogether. She did not respond when he called, though he tried only once and half-heartedly. What would the reporter think if Wilbur was rebuffed by his own wife? If he called and called and got no answer. Nobody would want to listen to a man whose own wife ignored him. What could someone like that have to say?

Wilbur assumed Sarah was seething upstairs or maybe hiding. She clearly wanted nothing to do with the brouhaha, and he couldn't blame her. He wanted nothing to do with the brouhaha either. But *he* didn't have a choice. There was no resentment in this. The interview did not need her. In fact, it probably would go more smoothly without her.

The question remained: what *was* he supposed to do. Should he make conversation? What if the man expected that? Maybe it would reflect poorly on Wilbur if he didn't say anything. The reporter probably had conducted thousands of interviews. Wilbur did not wish to be the first subject who failed to comport himself correctly.

"I've never done one of these before," he offered, acutely aware how trite the observation was.

The man ignored him, finished preparing for the interview, and took a deep breath. He clicked the recording device on, then thought better of it and clicked it off. Was this meant as a courtesy? Maybe it was his answer to Wilbur's comment, a kindness to the neophyte apprehensive about being recorded. Wilbur wondered whether his voice just wasn't pleasing enough.

Picking up pen and pad, the man began.

"Do you believe yourself at fault in all this?"

"I don't see how I could be," Wilbur replied. "It wasn't my choice."

"You were prompted then?"

"It was a misdelivery."

The man rubbed his chin for a moment. "Ah, I see. Indeed it was." He scribbled something. It was a lot of scribbling.

"Do you want to see?" Wilbur asked.

"The delivery?"

"The misdelivery."

The man thought briefly, then shook his head. "I've already heard that."

"You read my letter?"

"Everyone knows what happened."

This confused Wilbur. "I don't understand. I received no response, so I assumed—"

"Yes, you assumed." Scribble, scribble. "What was it precisely you assumed?"

"Well, that nobody was interested."

"You're not the first to make that assumption," the reporter observed. "It's a flawed one."

"There are others?"

The man smiled. "Well put. If you'd kept that in mind, this would have been easy to avoid."

"How?" It made little sense to Wilbur. If anything, the presence of others should indicate that such misdeliveries *weren't* easy to avoid.

"I think it is fair to say you've made quite the mess."

"But it wasn't me."

"That's what they always say. Or that they misspoke."

"I didn't misspeak," Wilbur insisted.

                    K.M. HALPERN

The man suddenly grew attentive. Apparently, this wasn't the expected response.

"Is something wrong?"

The man laughed with a snort. "Well, usually this is the part where you grovel and apologize. You really meant something else, didn't intend to offend anyone, and so on."

"I *didn't* intend to offend anyone."

"That's more like it," the man replied, once again detached.

"But I didn't *do* anything. How can anybody be offended?" Wilbur leaned in. "Did I breach protocol by calling the wrong people?"

"You certainly called the wrong people," the man laughed. He scribbled some more. Then he put down his pen and looked at Wilbur.

"I don't usually do this, but you seem utterly clueless. Do you know what your mistake was?"

Wilbur shook his head.

"You picked on the wrong professor. A professor of renown, true, but that's not it. Renown alone won't do it. Renowned professors don't bother swatting gnats. They don't need to."

This sounded insulting, but Wilbur said nothing.

"But this professor is, shall we say, the wrong type?"

"The wrong type?" Wilbur mumbled, uncertain what the man meant.

"The type who cannot be insulted. The type which always swats."

This made little sense to Wilbur. He had no idea what "type" the fellow was talking about. He didn't even know there *were* different types of professors.

Maybe they studied different subjects? Was that what the man meant? It still made no sense. There only was one professor Wilbur had spoken to, and she was friendly. She even loaned him a grad student. Who lends a grad student to someone they don't like?

"I didn't pick on any professor," Wilbur protested.

"Oh, but you did. You impugned the name of a professor. Not just any professor. The wrong professor."

"Is there a right professor to impugn?" Wilbur wondered aloud. Before the man could reply, he shook his head. "I didn't impugn anyone."

"It says so right here." The man thumbed through some pages. "Ah, you told Andrew Larick that you preferred to consult with someone else. That you were not comfortable with the professor's knowledge or competence. That you were not comfortable with *her*. Did you not say such a thing?"

"He said the professor didn't know the answer, but he knew somebody who may."

"And you went along with this ..." The man adopted an expression of distaste. "This farce."

"Farce? I don't see what's wrong."

"This ex-grad student—"

"Ex-grad student?" Had the professor foisted an ex-grad student on him? That felt cheap of her. Or maybe he still had been a grad student at the time. Did he graduate in the last two weeks? Wilbur had no idea what the academic schedule was like. It made him even more grateful. The poor man must have been so busy.

"This ex-grad student," the man repeated, "maligned his professor and you agreed. It was disrespectful, unprofessional, and unacceptable. Schools have a zero tolerance policy for that sort of thing."

"But he didn't, and I didn't."

"So, you didn't ask this Larick creature to take the matter to someone else?"

"As I said, he suggested it."

Scribble, scribble. The reporter looked at Wilbur. "Not a bad idea, shifting the blame. He's already guilty, so why not push it all onto him."

"That's not what I mean."

"We all know what you mean."

Wilbur stared at the man.

"Well, there you have it," the reporter explained as he rose. "There's only one way to interpret your actions. You clearly don't respect professors of this type."

"I really don't—"

The reporter scoffed. "It's shocking that in this day and age there still are people like you around." He clapped his hands together. "Well, the world's changing. Soon your kind will be gone." The man turned to leave.

"But I thought this was about the delivery," Wilbur protested.

"You claimed it was a misdelivery."

"Yes, the one I called you about."

The man smirked and sat down again. "Trying to get ahead of the scandal. I like it. Pretending you called me first."

"But I did. I told you about the device in my basement."

It was a few seconds before a glint of recognition crossed the reporter's face. "Oh yes, that guy." Suddenly he grew excited. "You're the same one? This will make good copy, after all."

Wilbur slumped back, relieved. It all had been a big misunderstanding.

"So you'll take a look."

The man glanced at his watch. "I'm here, so why not. It will provide a human interest angle. Maybe show your history of ..." He made an odd gesture with his hand and grinned at Wilbur. "You are a slippery one. It very well may work. I'm curious to see what happens."

The phone rang. Before Wilbur could pick up, the man reached over and snatched the handset. "I see, yes, I see."

Returning the phone to its cradle, the man quickly poured his effects into the briefcase. "Sorry, I have to run."

"But you said—"

"Wish I had time, but a certain celebrity was spotted drunk downtown." He winked at Wilbur. "You can guess who. If not, catch the five o'clock news."

"But what should I do?" Wilbur called out as the man sprinted for the door.

The man shrugged. "What else? Grovel and apologize."

Chapter 8

Despite their vehemence, the protesters had been surprisingly orderly. They mostly remained in the street, and there was no vandalism. They even picked up their litter. The only casualty was Sarah's garden, and that was the fault of reporters. Those were not conscientious about anything.

Though Wilbur dared not downplay the injury to his wife's petunias, all in all he felt lucky. Mere hours after the chaos, it would have been hard to imagine anything had transpired.

However, the affair did drive home one important point. He was exposed. *They* were exposed. Wilbur's insurance was not nearly enough to cover anything serious. The policy hadn't been updated in some time and probably didn't reflect the present value of the house. It certainly did not account for the thing in the basement and what could happen because of it. Or to it.

In fact, Wilbur was unsure whether rioting was covered at all. He felt it should be, but what he felt was of little consequence. Who would decide such a thing? What if that person was one of the rioters? This struck him as unlikely — the rioters were too young to have attained that level of responsibility — but he could not dismiss the possibility.

The biggest question was that of money. Wilbur was uncertain how large a policy to get. His main concerns were theft and damage, not liability. If the device went off, he would be beyond the purview of the courts. But what if someone stole or damaged it? If the protesters had been of the more unruly variety, that could have happened. And just because he couldn't figure out a way to remove the thing didn't mean an enterprising burglar wouldn't. Young people could be quite resourceful when properly motivated.

Wilbur had to admit that the prospect of such a theft was not entirely unappealing. If the device was stolen, it wouldn't be his problem anymore. He would be a victim, beyond blame. If a famous artwork was misdelivered and then stolen, would the recipient be liable?

Actually, he was unclear on this point. It would be unfair, but fairness and the law had little to do with one another. It wasn't Wilbur's fault that his house was not secure. He hadn't ordered the device or even expected it. But would they care? They'd probably think he stole it. There just were too many if's. He couldn't place his hope in serendipity. When had serendipity ever been his friend? He only could rely on himself, and it was clear how well that worked.

At least he could limit his financial exposure. The last thing he needed was to get sued for reimbursement by the real owner. The thought made Wilbur mad. He should be getting reimbursed *by* the owner for all the trouble they had caused. But that never would happen. It just wasn't how the world worked. Everyone knew that the victim always paid.

This raised an interesting question. How much was the thing actually worth? Certainly more than he could afford. It would be good to know that number before someone actually demanded it of him. But how would the owner know whom to sue? If they knew he had the device, surely they'd have collected it by now. What if Erik was right, and he was the true owner. Would he have to sue himself?

Even if the device was intended for him, what if it just was on loan? Maybe the whole thing was a big test, some social experiment to see whether he would press the button. The owners eventually would want to retrieve the thing, so they could pass it along to someone else. Wilbur wondered whether they would have their own insurance in that case.

But theft wasn't the only threat or even the biggest. Removing the device would require ingenuity but damaging it would not. The thing looked solid enough, but that didn't mean it was indestructible. For all Wilbur knew, the mechanism was incredibly delicate. In fact, this seemed quite likely in light of Andrew's explanation. Why else the heavy crate, the robust mount, the dense packing material?

Wilbur flirted with each individual worry to one degree or another, but a principal anxiety soon emerged. What if someone stole the control box? That would be easy to accomplish and would render the device inoperable. Then he'd be stuck with the thing forever. Who would bother to retrieve a piece of inoperable junk?

Nor was the issue of liability completely moot. Detonation wasn't the only hazard attending the device. What if a protester tripped or a reporter injured himself? He'd read of a case where a burglar sued and won. A few million for an injured toe, Wilbur recalled. He wondered how such numbers were arrived at. Why was one toe worth millions and another worth nothing?

In Wilbur's experience, when something seemed arbitrary it simply meant he did not know the principle. If he knew the principle, it wouldn't seem arbitrary. Wilbur hoped these unknown principles would work in his favor but was certain they would not. He reluctantly decided to increase his liability insurance.

It would cost a bit extra but was worth it. Wilbur needed to be well-insured, protected, unexposed. He suddenly grew nervous. What if something happened before he could get the new policy? Maybe the protest was just an opening volley. Would all those people reappear the next day and the next? Had they picked up their litter because they intended to return? It made sense. Nobody would want to protest in yesterday's trash.

Wilbur could not rely on such propriety. The protesters could grow more rowdy each day. Or different ones could appear. Different and violent. Insurance only could protect him financially, but it somehow made him feel physically safer as well.

Wilbur shared some, but not all, of these thoughts with Sarah. She was uninterested in most, but the matter of liability got her attention. Her only reply was that it better not cost too much. Wilbur promised it wouldn't, knowing that whatever it did cost would be too much.

Getting through to the insurance company was easier than Wilbur expected. The agent's number was on his current policy, and she picked up on the first ring. He explained that he wanted to increase the policy's limits.

"Why?" she asked.

"Well, I'd like to be protected." Wilbur hadn't expected an interrogation. Why did they care? He had assumed they would be glad to take his money.

"So you're planning to do something risky?"

"No," Wilbur insisted, "I just feel exposed."

"I see, you expose yourself. We don't provide legal help if you're arrested."

"No, legally exposed."

"I don't think you legally can expose yourself. Are you an adult entertainer?"

Wilbur had no idea how the conversation had taken this turn. "Look, I haven't updated my policy in some time. I just want to make sure I'm covered."

"Then don't expose yourself," the woman suggested.

Wilbur hung up and redialed the number. The woman picked up on the first ring.

"I'd like to increase the limit on my current policy," Wilbur explained.

"Why?" she asked.

"I have something expensive that needs insuring."

"Something specific?"

"Yes."

"Do you know what it is?"

Wilbur sighed. No point being coy.

"A 1.72 megaton nuclear bomb."

There was a pause, and he waited for the dial-tone. Instead he heard some rustling, then some chewing.

"I don't have that in the catalog. We'll need to have it appraised."

"Appraised?"

"Someone will need to be home. I can give you a morning or afternoon slot."

"What day?"

"Today's Monday."

"What day will the appraiser come?" Wilbur clarified.

"Don't know. Morning or afternoon?"

"When's soonest?"

"It's morning now, so probably afternoon?"

"You can send him today?"

"I never said that."

Wilbur took a deep breath. "Afterno— no, morning."

"I entered afternoon."

"Whe—"

"Three weeks from Wednesday."

"Bu—"

There was a dial-tone.

Wilbur dialed the number again, and the woman picked up.

"I didn't tell you who I am."

"That would be the polite thing to do," she observed.

"You'll also need my address."

"Why?"

After repeating the entire conversation word for word, Wilbur asked her to confirm the appointment date.

"Four weeks from Tuesday."

"I thought you said three weeks from Wednes-day."

"I just filled that slot."

Sarah was not pleased. She did not like the idea of an appraisal. Wilbur thought it odd that she had no problem with unsupervised deliverymen but balked at an insurance appraiser. Wouldn't he be less likely to steal something? He certainly would know what was worth stealing, so perhaps the opposite was true. It didn't matter. They needed the appraisal.

Nonetheless, Wilbur felt uneasy as well. They were about to be judged. A stranger would come into their home and calculate their worth, the sum total of their value in this world. Was there any difference between appraising a man and what he owned? He wondered whether this was the real reason behind Sarah's opposition. The thought warmed him. It would be nice if they had something in common.

Sarah was in a terrible mood the rest of the day. It didn't help that the appraiser showed up the very next morning, just as Wilbur was about to leave for work.

Wilbur stood dumbfounded in the doorway.

"I'm here for the appraisal," the man repeated.

"I thought it was four weeks from Tuesday."

"Today is Tuesday, so it *is* four weeks from a

Tuesday."

Wilbur did not know what to say and let the man in.

"I'm sorry, I didn't catch your name," he said, guiding the appraiser down the hall and dreading Sarah's reaction. At least she already was awake and dressed.

"I didn't throw it," the man replied.

"Throw what?"

"It was a joke." The man held out his hand. "Burt."

Wilbur shook it just as Sarah emerged from the kitchen. Seeing the man, she adjusted her hair and smiled. It wasn't the reaction Wilbur had expected, and he decided to stick around for the inspection. Then he remembered that he had to anyway. Who else would show him the device?

Sarah whisked Burt away and gave him a tour of the house. The man seemed a bit puzzled but was a good sport. Wilbur told himself he didn't mind. It probably just was the excitement of having a guest. Was Sarah bored and lonely most of the time? He felt like he knew the answer to this but never could hang on to it. Maybe the appraiser reminded her of a beloved relative. In any case, it was better than having her browbeat the fellow. The last thing they needed was a vindictive appraiser.

"I'll be downstairs," Wilbur called out, but there was no reply. He spent the time tidying up the area around the device.

When he heard the voice of the man in the kitchen, Wilbur reemerged.

"Did you see everything you needed to?" he

asked. Sarah gave him a sour look. Wilbur hadn't intended it as a pointed question.

Burt nodded and began to zip up his satchel.

"There's one more thing," Wilbur said. "It's in the basement."

The appraiser seemed hesitant.

"That won't be necessary. In my experience, there's never anything interesting in the basement." He looked at them both. "From a monetary standpoint I mean — whatever the sentimental value may be."

Why avoid the basement? Surely, an appraiser regularly went into basements. Did he think Wilbur was a jealous husband hoping to ambush him? Or maybe he thought they both were crazy.

"The item I want appraised is downstairs," Wilbur explained.

"I thought this was a general appraisal."

"Well, I called about a specific item."

"That wasn't conveyed to me." Burt consulted his notes. "Nope, nothing specific."

"Since you're here, can you appraise it anyway? It was the reason I called."

Burt looked uneasy. "This is most irregular."

His eyes flitted between Sarah and Wilbur. "I can look at it as part of the general appraisal, but it won't be a scheduled item."

"It still will be covered?" Wilbur didn't care about the specifics, as long as he wasn't exposed.

"It will." Burt grew serious. "Just to confirm: you want me to go into the basement during a general appraisal?"

"Yeah. Why?"

The man grimaced ever so slightly. "Most people don't."

"Well, I do."

This seemed to dispel Burt's reticence. He shrugged and followed Wilbur into the basement without further objection.

—•—

One week later, a letter from the insurance company arrived.

"Insurance Denied," it read, followed by some impenetrable jargon. Wilbur dialed the agent.

"Why was my insurance denied?"

"I don't know. Was it with us?"

"Of course."

Before she could reply, he gave her the account number.

"There's no such account, I'm afraid."

"We spoke last week," Wilbur insisted.

"Nice to hear from you again."

"Can you look me up by name?"

"Sorry, I can't do that."

Wilbur groaned but then had an idea.

"Here, I'll read you the letter."

"You wrote a letter?"

"No, you did. To me."

"I think I would remember that."

"Let me read it, and you'll see," Wilbur explained.

"Why would you read my own letter back to me? Did I make a mistake?"

"Yes, you denied me insurance."

"That sounds like a decision not a mistake. There's a difference, I think."

"Just listen!" Wilbur read the letter.

"Oh, I see. You've been denied insurance."

"That's the problem. You even canceled my existing policy."

"Well, you can't have two policies with us."

"I don't have any!"

"Then you should apply. Can I interest you in some sales literature?"

"Why was I denied?" Wilbur demanded.

"I thought the letter was clear."

"It didn't make sense," he complained.

"Well, let's see. It said that the insurable value was too high."

"I don't understand."

"It would cost too much to insure you. We can't underwrite it."

Wilbur thought about this. "Because of the device?"

"What device?" She thought for a moment. "Oh, I see. Yes, there was one item with an extremely high value. It's listed in the letter."

Wilbur scanned the document and found the number. It took a while to properly count the number of zeroes.

"It can't possibly be worth that much," he protested, almost shouting.

"No, that would be the cost to insure it."

A bit more scanning led to another number. It took even longer to count the zeroes on this one. So *that* was the appraised value. There was no way he could afford to insure it. Wilbur's stomach sank.

He would have to remain exposed. Worse, even the slightest scratch on something so valuable would be more than he could afford. His mind immediately began to downplay the very risks which seemed unavoidable moments earlier. With a sigh, he asked the agent to remove the device from his insurance.

"I'm afraid that is impossible."

"What do you mean? I just want to go back to the old policy," he explained.

"We only can remove scheduled items. Since it was part of a general appraisal, it is inseparable from the whole."

"Can you pretend it doesn't exist?"

"Can you?"

Wilbur conceded that he could not. If he could, none of this would be necessary.

"Then I'm sorry, there's nothing we can do."

"Can I have another appraisal?" Wilbur didn't relish the thought of a second visit from Burt, but it was better than being without insurance.

"There would be no point. Once we know the overall value we cannot unknow it."

"Then I'll take my business elsewhere," Wilbur replied in a huff. It sounded far less threatening than intended.

"Appraisals are shared between insurers," the woman explained. "Everybody will give you the same answer."

"Isn't there anything we can do?" Wilbur pleaded. "I must be able to get insurance somehow."

"I'm afraid not. The only way ... "

"Yes?" Wilbur eagerly prompted.

"... would be to get rid of the high-value item."

Chapter 9

A few days later, Wilbur returned from work to find Sarah in the doorway, arms crossed, face a practiced frown. She announced that she had been counting the minutes until he got home. Had she been standing like that all day or did she wait for the sound of his car? And why hadn't she just called him at work?

They did have that thing in the basement, even if she refused to discuss it. Had she gone down there while he was away? Wilbur grew anxious. Maybe she really knew who delivered it. Maybe it was meant for her, and she feigned indifference. He hadn't considered that. Wilbur liked to believe there would have been some sign during their many years of marriage that she was a spy or terrorist or whatever undefinable suspicion was forming in his mind. What exactly *did* he imagine her to be?

Sarah waved an empty envelope.

"Do you know what this is?" she demanded with a pout that made Wilbur want to kiss her.

What was she talking about? Sarah must have been pleased by Wilbur's dumbfounded expression, and she grinned. It wasn't a warm grin.

"I'm sure I can take care of it, just let me have a look," Wilbur offered. It seemed the easiest way out of whatever this was. Maybe the letter was about the device. He suddenly grew hopeful.

"I tore it up," Sarah snapped, turning on her heels.

"But—"

"I told you to get rid of the damned thing," she griped over her shoulder.

The damned thing? Wilbur couldn't imagine she referred to anything other than the device. But wasn't this about a letter? Maybe that meant it wasn't about the device, though Wilbur had a horrible suspicion it was. Sarah shouldn't have torn the letter up. Anger briefly overcame his concern for her temper. He was about to confront her but recalled how upset she had seemed. Had there been a soft redness around her eyes?

Wilbur hadn't given much thought to how the device affected Sarah, just how to get rid of it. It was in his basement, and he had come to regard it as his problem. But she had to live with the thing all day every day. At least he got time away from it. Wilbur began to sense the strain she was under. But that was a general consideration, and he had more specific ones to worry about at the moment.

He scrambled for a way to calm things as he followed his wife into the living room. It was difficult without having read the letter. At best he could argue that he'd tried to involve her but she refused, that either she should leave everything to him or help out.

As it happened, Wilbur was not called upon to deploy this or any other defense. Sarah did not return to the topic, and Wilbur feared to raise it. He wondered whether she sensed his readiness to push back. She would wait until he was unready, off-guard, had forgotten his defense, or had no hope of mustering it in time. The argument would be on her terms. It always was.

All day, Wilbur waited on tenterhooks for the onslaught. As much as he wished to learn what was in the letter, he dared not ask. It was a matter of simple self-preservation. To prematurely unleash Sarah's fury would be pointless. Even if he managed to placate her it would be temporary, a mere rehearsal which would not dampen the true storm in the slightest.

To Wilbur's surprise, the tempest did not materialize that evening or the next. In fact, his wife was unusually agreeable. Perhaps she felt guilty for destroying the letter. It seemed doubtful, but hope always was.

One day the following week, Wilbur returned home to find the house empty. A small note rested atop a grocery bag filled with mail. Sarah would be visiting her sister for a while. When she returned, she expected that "it would be cleared up."

Her meaning was unambiguous. Sarah was not close to her sister, either geographically or emotionally. When she visited her, there was a purpose. It was a tactic she employed sparingly, one kept in reserve as a calculated escalation.

The note unsettled Wilbur more than Sarah's departure. She never left a note, and he always had to ferret out why she left. That was part of his penance. It wasn't like Sarah to be straightforward. Was this a testament to how angry she had become? Was this time different? Perhaps that was the real message.

He suspected Sarah left partly from fear of exploding at him. Despite her occasional temper, she possessed a certain decorum. Her fusillades were controlled. Perhaps even planned, though Wilbur never had been sure. Either way, there were rules they followed. Or rules she made them follow. Perhaps this time she could not count on such restraint.

How had he made her that mad? He hadn't done anything. Well, that did seem to be the problem. He *hadn't* done anything. Or at least he hadn't accomplished anything. The two were quite different, though perhaps not to her mind. Sarah at least should have credited him with trying. She had been there when he called and called and called. It wasn't his fault that nobody was willing to listen. Or that the insurance policy had been lost. Well, maybe that was his fault. Wilbur still hadn't decided where the blame lay.

Misgivings aside, he had mixed feelings about Sarah's absence. It would be nice to have the house to himself. Dealing with the device would be easier absent an irascible boss. Was that how he viewed her? Why did he stay with her if that's all she was? Did he *want* that? Wilbur decided, as he always did when it came to such things, that now wasn't the time. There were more pressing matters. And for once, there actually were.

Even with the run of the house, what would he do? Wilbur now had an ultimatum, though he suspected and hoped and was somewhat sure it really wasn't one. She would stay away a bit longer than usual or come back and vent at him, but things eventually would return to normal. Probably.

There was nothing he could do about that at the moment, not directly. What he *could* do was address the reason for her departure. But there was a problem: he had no idea what that reason was. In its own odd way, this was comforting. Sarah *had* left him clueless, note notwithstanding. Maybe this time was just like all the rest.

That didn't make his task any easier. Nor could he await clarification. Even without an ultimatum, dealing with the issue now would be easier than when she returned. Still, it was hard to focus while he imagined her hating him from afar. That probably was what she wanted.

Wilbur decided to sift through the mail. He always found that relaxing. The mail held infinite possibility. There could be an unhoped-for letter from some old friend or a check for a huge sum or maybe an invitation to some grand affair. That such things hadn't happened didn't mean they couldn't. The mail was a conduit to fate, and he just had to have faith. Wilbur glanced at the wall-clock. An hour or two wouldn't make any difference, and perhaps it would help clear his mind.

As he opened the bag of mail, Wilbur wondered why Sarah had troubled to pack it this way. Usually, letters just sat in a naked pile on the credenza. Maybe it was intended as a statement of some sort. He pulled out the first letter.

It was from an agency he'd never heard of. Probably a water bill or something. He tore open the envelope.

"First Notice of Tax Assessment." This puzzled him. They'd just had a tax assessment. The notice had to be a misdelivery, and he hoped such things wouldn't become a regular occurrence. Had he become a magnet for misdeliveries? Maybe people knew he was the type of guy who could be misdelivered to.

Wilbur glanced at the address being assessed. It was indeed his. Why did they need another tax assessment? It seemed wasteful. His eyes scanned the page until he came across a numeric value. Wilbur slumped onto the couch in relief. It was an obvious mistake. The number was far too large to be correct.

What he first thought was a tax assessment must have been a general notice, one of those city budget statements which explained the overall disposition of tax revenue. That would explain the huge number. He always liked to know how his taxes were spent and decided to peruse the document. It wasn't a budget statement.

Sales tax? On what? He already knew the answer. Wilbur felt a mixture of panic and indignation. How could they charge tax on something that wasn't his? He had tried to get rid of the thing, had done everything right. How did they even know he had it, let alone how much it was worth?

The dollar figure looked vaguely familiar. Checking his notes, Wilbur realized it was precisely the value assigned by Burt. The insurance company must have forwarded their appraisal to the state. It seemed like a mean-spirited thing to do. Maybe they were legally obligated to?

Why hadn't anybody at the tax office taken exception to the high number? Surely, it should have raised a flag. Perhaps he could call and convince them of the absurdity of the figure. He'd say it was a glitch, some sort of obvious error. Then they'd have a good laugh, and the charge would be expunged.

For the first time since the assessment, Wilbur considered the actual appraised value. Did people really traffic in such figures? An unworthy thought began to form, but he quashed it. Even if he was that sort of person, Wilbur had no idea how to go about it. If he couldn't even find someone to take the thing for free, how would he convince anyone to pay an obscene sum for that same privilege. And he'd probably have to pay an impossible tax on the transaction. Would the seller or the buyer pay it? Maybe he just could donate the damned thing.

Maybe he *could* donate it. Wilbur felt a burst of hope. People donated old junkers and other things which were tough to remove. There must be charities which would come and collect such items. Wilbur wasn't sure of the specifics, but it seemed a good way out of the whole mess. Surely they couldn't tax him on something he didn't own. Maybe he'd even come out ahead if he got a hefty deduction out of it. But first things first. Wilbur was starving.

He wandered into the kitchen. With Sarah gone, it no longer felt off limits. Besides, he had to eat. It turned out to be a moot point. The refrigerator was empty, and there was nothing in the oven. It was too late for the grocery store, so Wilbur decided to call it a night. He slept on the couch. The bed just didn't feel right without Sarah.

First thing the next day, Wilbur researched charities. There was one likely candidate in the area.

"Ben Sharitz Hillel charities." The man on the other end sounded chipper.

"Do you take unwanted things?"

"Only if they aren't grumpy."

It took a moment for Wilbur to realize it was a joke. He didn't laugh. "I have something to donate."

"We can help with that too," the man quipped.

"Will you collect it?"

"We can arrange for collection. Do you have a model?"

Wilbur asked the man to hold and quickly retrieved the manual. He rattled off the 34 digits of the serial number.

"Are you sure that's the model number?" the man asked. "It seems long for one, and I don't recognize it."

After searching the manual, Wilbur spotted another number. This one had 22 digits. He read it to the man but was greeted with silence.

"Hello," he ventured.

"I'm afraid we can't help you."

"Why?" Wilbur asked. "Do you know what it is?"

"Of course. You gave me the model number. It's correct, I assume?"

"Yes," he replied, reviewing the code to make sure. "Yep, just as I said."

"Then, I'm afraid we cannot take it."

"It's worth a lot."

"Then why donate it?"

Wilbur hadn't been prepared for this question. "I don't know. It just appeared, and I need to get rid of it."

"Well, there is one easy way to get rid of it."

"What's that?" Wilbur asked before realizing it was another joke. A joke in remarkably poor taste. Unless the man was mistaken or just pretending. Maybe he actually had no idea what the device was.

"What do you think I'm talking about?" he asked the man.

"I think you're talking about what you *are* talking about. It wouldn't make much sense to think you are talking about something else."

"I mean, can you repeat to me the description corresponding to the model I gave you."

"I'm afraid we're not a catalog service."

"Please, I just need to know." Wilbur wasn't sure why he was so adamant about confirming this, but it felt important.

"You don't know what it is? How can you have something and not know what it is? Do you actually have the thing?"

"I do."

"Then why do you need me to tell you what you have?"

"Isn't there anything you can do?" Wilbur asked. "I really need to get rid of it."

"Well, how did you get it?"

"It was delivered."

"Have you tried returning it to the sender? That's where I would start."

Wilbur began to explain, but the man interrupted. "I'm sorry, I have another caller. Please feel free to call back with any other donation questions."

Only after hanging up did Wilbur realize he'd finally found someone who knew about the device. Instead of pointless verification, why hadn't he asked him about the thing? Who produced it, where to send it. He had missed a critical opportunity. No, not missed. All he needed to do was call back. The man had suggested he do so if he had any other questions.

A different man picked up. This time, he didn't recognize the model.

"But I just spoke to one of your guys. He knew what I was talking about."

"Do you know who it was?"

Wilbur hadn't thought to ask the man's name.

"I'm afraid not," he explained. "But it should be pretty easy to tell. I just called a few minutes ago."

"I can't help you without the name," the man explained.

"What is your name?" Wilbur asked without thinking.

"That won't help since I'm not the man you spoke with."

Wilbur felt dizzy and a little bit nauseous.

"Isn't there someone who knows these things. Someone senior?"

"We're a charity, not a company. There are no ranks, and everyone is a volunteer."

"Can you ask around?" Wilbur pleaded.

"I'm sorry. If you want to call back, you may get him."

"Will I?"

"Probably not. We're a big organization."

"Isn't there anything I can do? I really need his help," Wilbur insisted.

"And he said we could help you?"

"No, he said you can't take it. But he knew what it was."

"Then you have your answer. If he said we can't take it, what more is there to know?"

"Pleas—" Wilbur began, but the line went dead. Over the next two days Wilbur tried again numerous times, with similar success.

Only toward the end of the second day did Wilbur recall that there was somebody else with knowledge of the device. The appraiser must have possessed some means of estimating its value. Maybe he too had a catalog and could provide information. Wilbur was loathe to make the call, but two things decided him.

First, Sarah was away. If for some reason the man had to visit, there would be nothing to worry about. Had he been worried? Wilbur wondered about this and felt lessened for doing so. But the more compelling reason was that the man owed him. After causing the tax fiasco, the least Burt could do was help him out.

Wilbur called the insurance company.

"As I told you sir, we cannot insure you," the woman warned before Wilbur could say anything.

"It's not that."

"You wish to dispute the assessment?" Her voice

had a slightly confrontational tone.

"No."

"I can't help you, then." She hung up.

The second attempt went roughly the same way. On the third try, Wilbur replied that yes, he would like to dispute the valuation.

"I'll need to send you an appeal form, and you will have to arrange for an apprai—"

"That's fine. Incidentally, I was wondering whether I could get in touch with the appraiser."

"I can't give out employee information."

"I really need to speak with him," Wilbur insisted.

The woman hung up. He decided on another approach and tried again, repeating the conversation verbatim up to the scheduling of the appraiser.

"I know it's an unusual request, but my wife is very skittish about having people in the house."

"We need to conduct an appraisal, sir."

"Well, she really liked the fellow you sent last time. Short guy, mustache—"

"I have the records, sir."

Wilbur tried not to be put off by the perfunctory, almost impatient, tone of the woman's responses. By now he had been dealing with them for over two hours.

"I'd really appreciate it if you could send him out again."

"I'm not sure we can accommodate that, sir."

"Can you try?" he wheedled. "Why else would I want the same guy? You denied me insurance last time, so it's obviously disadvantageous to me."

There was a pause.

"I'll see what I can do."

Wilbur thanked her and hung up.

It wasn't until the next day that the phone rang. Wilbur dashed for it, struggling to sound calm as he cradled the receiver.

"Hello."

"Tryant."

"Sorry, Tryant who?"

"You asked for me," the man explained, identifying the insurance company. Wilbur was caught off guard. He hadn't expected the appraiser himself to call. "Burt?" he asked hesitantly.

"Yes, Burt Tryant. But let's keep to Mr. Tryant. It sounds more professional."

Wilbur was too delighted to fret over such inconsequentialities. "That's great," he blubbered. "So great. Thanks for calling back."

"It's my job."

Wilbur found himself at a loss for words.

"You want to dispute my appraisal?" the man prompted.

"No, no. I want a new appraisal."

"Oh, in that case, I'll connect you with—"

"Wait, wait, please," Wilbur begged, clutching the phone with painful intensity.

"Ok."

"You appraised the item. How did you know about it?"

"It's my job to know about such things. Are you questioning my judgment?"

"No, no. I just need to know about it."

There was a pause, and Wilbur dreaded a dial-tone. Instead the man's voice issued. He sounded surprised.

"Is this a joke? You have it, so why do you need to be told about it?"

Wilbur haltingly explained how it had been misdelivered and that he was trying to contact the manufacturer or somebody. Anybody.

"I'm afraid I can't give out that information. It could be misused."

"But how? I already have the device."

"If you were meant to be privy to such information, I'm sure you would be. Did you read the manual?"

"I looked it over. The part that's in English says nothing. The rest I can't read."

"I'm sorry, but maybe you can hire a translation service."

Wilbur was almost in tears. "But I don't even know what language to try."

"I'm afraid that's not my domain of expertise, sir."

"Can't you tell me *anything*?"

There was a long silence, and Wilbur wondered what the man was thinking. Was he thinking? Maybe he was watching TV and had forgotten to hang up. Burt's voice finally emerged from the ether.

"Make sure you understand the manual before using it. And don't try to disassemble it. You're not covered for loss, and you'll want that warranty intact."

"But—"

"Please feel free to contact the insurance company with any other questions."

The line went dead. That seemed to happen a lot.

—•—

Now that his hopes had been dashed, Wilbur fell into a quiet desperation. His attention returned to the bag of letters, unopened and waiting. He had forgotten about them and felt quite the fool to have imagined they entailed a single crisis. If every other letter were equally problematic, there would be no hope of salvation. The trouble would be insurmountable. No wonder Sarah fled!

They already were in dire straits, and Wilbur did not wish to imagine how much worse things could get. Judging by the size of the bag, there were at least a dozen more landmines inside. After a great deal of procrastination, he decided it was better to know than not.

"Zoning Violation and Requirement for Remediation." That his home was not zoned for military use wasn't a surprise. The hefty fine was.

"State Mandate for Minimal Insurance." The penalty was a fixed, modest amount, but the principle annoyed Wilbur as much as the rest. Perhaps even more so because this was a sum he plausibly could be expected to pay.

"Military Enterprise Registration Act." Apparently, he was required to register any private large-scale military venture. Wilbur wondered how many large-scale military ventures there were and who registered them. Registration seemed against the spirit of such things. Why not demand a license as well? As if in reply, the next letter did.

"License Violation for Military Enterprise." Wilbur briefly wondered what sort of penalty accrued to those who embarked on unlicensed military enterprises. Apparently, a substantial fine and possible criminal charges. Were they serious about this or did it fall in the same camp as jury duty and minor tax fudges? How would they even penalize a military enterprise? Maybe with another military enterprise. Would that require a license too? Wilbur envisioned an endless chain of military enterprises, each punishing the previous.

"Import Tariff", **"Nonunion Delivery Assessment"**, **"Failure to Inspect Product"**, **"No Declaration of Employee Benefits on File"**, and on and on. Most were complaints, demands for paperwork, or sternly-worded warnings of potential court action. A few were more substantive or puzzling.

"Violation of Technology Import." Despite the banal heading, this was one of the most worrisome. It meant Wilbur really could go to jail. From what he'd read, the State Department took a dim view of people who exported restricted technologies. It stood to reason that the same would be true of imports. The complaint itself was a jumble of technical jargon, and Wilbur did not recognize the offending chemicals. After a careful rereading — and based on the stated volume, size, and description — he concluded that it must refer to the packing material.

"FCC Consumer Device Noncompliance." It

seemed quite reasonable there would be concerns about radiation from a nuclear bomb, though Andrew had assured Wilbur there wasn't any. It took a few readings of the acronym-laden letter before he realized the complaint was about something else entirely. The noncompliant device was the little control box. It was unclear whether it operated in a forbidden portion of the spectrum or simply failed to declare what portion of the spectrum it did operate in.

"Agriculture Act Failure to Mitigate." Of all the letters, this puzzled Wilbur the most. At first he assumed it was a mistake. Maybe with so many agencies complaining at once, this somehow slipped in undetected. To his dismay, it had not. The crate was made from a rare hardwood which was susceptible to infestation by a certain invasive weevil. Proof of treatment had not been filed. This struck Wilbur as uncharacteristically careless of the sender. He almost laughed. Uncharacteristically careless? He wouldn't be in this mess if they had been anything *but* uncharacteristically careless. Or at least careless. He could not reasonably attest to whether such carelessness was characteristic or uncharacteristic of them. Come to think of it, had other misdeliveries been made? Maybe his neighbors had similar devices in their basements. It was a disturbing prospect. Wilbur did not trust his neighbors. Most didn't take proper care of their lawns.

"Notice of Reassessment and Tax Lien." The presence of the device had triggered a reassessment of the value of Wilbur's home. But why would the value of his home be affected by the things in it, let alone the device? It took nearly an hour of digging through abstruse legalese before he began to understand the issue. They weren't assessing the item as part of the house, though its immobility apparently also put him at risk of that. The logic was that any dwelling which adequately could house such a high-value item must have been designed and built with that item in mind, and thus have a correspondingly high intrinsic value. This made sense to Wilbur in a perverse sort of way. From his warehouse days he knew that expensive items had expensive cases. Those cases often were no better than the inexpensive cases which came with inexpensive items, but that didn't make them any less expensive.

In total, Wilbur had to contend with almost forty notices, warnings, and complaints. He was impressed Sarah managed to fit them in a single plastic bag. Or even separate them from the other mail. They hadn't been opened, so how did she know which was which? What if there were others she didn't recognize as such? He decided it didn't matter. It would be no easier to get out from under a hundred tons than two hundred tons. Or 1.72 megatons.

Chapter 10

After a great deal of dithering, Wilbur decided to contact a realtor. There were many reasons not to sell the house and only one reason to. It was a compelling reason but wasn't why he called. He called because he had to do *something*. A call cost nothing, bound him to nothing. Speaking with a realtor was a far cry from selling the house. Knowing his options couldn't hurt, especially since he had no idea what Sarah intended. Maybe she would be pleased with his initiative.

When Wilbur opened the door, the realtor did not enter right away. She stood on the stoop with expectant eyes and a plastic smile. Was Wilbur supposed to do something, say something, offer something? Then he noticed that her eyes weren't on him; they were fixed on the hall behind him. The expression was unmistakable.

"My wife's away," he explained. "It's just me."

"Ah."

This single word carried more condescension than Sarah's most potent smirk. Wilbur was impressed. Was this what it meant to be a maestro?

After a moment, the woman extended her hand. "Sheila."

Her handshake was limp, and Wilbur briefly wondered whether he was supposed to kiss it. He had no desire to do so. She was here to discuss his house, not have her hand kissed.

Wilbur remembered his old realtor, the one who sold him the place many years earlier. He wondered whether she still was around. Her name was Sheila too, and he had not kissed her hand either. Would things have gone better if he had? Maybe he would have bought a different house. Then somebody else would be in this position. Or perhaps the device would have been delivered to him anyway. Were all wrong destinations really the same?

This woman was not the same Sheila. For one thing, she was too young. Not young, just too young. Were all realtors named Sheila, or did they grow into that name? Maybe it was adopted when they started the job, like a pope or king.

Wilbur invited Sheila in, but she motioned him outside.

"Best to take a look while we're already out here."

Wilbur wasn't already out there, but he chose not to argue the point. If that's what was best, he would do it. It always was best to do what was best. The alternative rarely was appealing. After putting on shoes, he joined her in the front yard.

It was not at all obvious from Sheila's varying demeanor and occasional muttering what she thought, but at length Wilbur surmised that she was pleased. This puzzled him. Why would a realtor be pleased or displeased? It wasn't her house. She just had to determine the right price.

Maybe it was a carefully guarded secret that all houses actually were the same price. Wilbur wondered whether the whole thing was an elaborate charade to make her appear useful. If so, she could spare herself the trouble. He didn't need to be convinced. It probably made no difference which realtor he picked, so he may as well pick her. Especially if they all were Sheilas anyway.

—•—

Sheila spent little time outside but a great deal studying the kitchen and bathrooms. Wilbur was unsure whether this meant the outside was easy to appraise or she just didn't like the weather. It didn't matter to him where she spent her time. The house was just a house, other than the thing in the basement.

Wilbur allowed Sheila a respectable amount of time before intruding with questions. At least he deemed it a respectable amount of time. He had little sense of what was or was not respectable in such a situation. Sheila paid him no mind.

For a while, the realtor darted to and fro, examining this and that, and entirely ignoring Wilbur's presence. He wondered whether it would be the same if Sarah were home. Would the two women have bonded? Maybe Sarah would be more aggressive. Should he try to sell Sheila on the house? It seemed silly to have to sell her on something she would be selling. If he knew how to sell the house, he wouldn't need a realtor.

When Wilbur sensed Sheila was winding down, he once again ventured to ask her thoughts.

There was a pensive silence before she replied. "It's a house."

"What is it worth?"

"That depends who you ask."

"I'm asking you." He felt the beginning of a headache.

She shrugged. "A six percent commission."

"No, I mean what is it worth to me?" Why did he have such trouble making himself understood these days? Had it always been such a struggle?

Sheila seemed confused. "Protection, privacy, storage, memories? I imagine it's worth a lot to you since you live here. Though you *are* selling, so maybe not."

"I mean the price. What price can we sell it for?"

"Oh, I see." She gave him an annoyed look. "Then why didn't you say that? It's much easier to determine something's price than its worth."

"I'm saying it now." Wilbur worried he was being too assertive. Would antagonizing the realtor lower the price? Maybe she would refuse to sell it at all. There were others, but if he offended one he'd probably offend them all. Maybe all the Sheilas really were one Sheila.

To his relief she did not appear offended, just perplexed. Speaking as if to a child, she explained. "Well we won't know the price until somebody buys it."

"But how do you know what to ask for it?"

"You mean how do I get somebody to buy it?" Again, Sheila seemed unclear on what he meant. "That's what a good realtor does. A bad realtor doesn't get anybody to buy it."

Wilbur was about to ask whether she was a "good realtor" but realized she hadn't yet been downstairs. Good or bad, a realtor couldn't be expected to sell the house without seeing what was in the basement. He hoped it wouldn't affect the price but was certain it would.

Maybe it would raise the price, like buried treasure. Except that it wasn't buried and it wasn't treasure. Was it? Wilbur wondered whether he was looking at it the wrong way. Looking at things the wrong way had been a growing concern these last two months. Maybe he was looking at *everything* the wrong way.

"Let me show you the basement," he suggested.

Sheila shook her head. "No need. Nobody buys a house for the basement."

"But what if there is flooding or the heater is broken?"

The realtor gave him a concerned glance.

"There isn't," he promised. "But there's something else."

"Is it part of the house?"

"Sort of. It weighs a lot."

"Well, we'll just make sure the contract covers that."

Wilbur's eyes widened. Why hadn't he thought of that. If the buyer didn't openly object, he would be relieved of the problem. A moment later this hope was dashed.

"It's obligatory for the seller to remove all unattached possessions."

"I'm certainly not attached to it." He wondered whether this was true.

"Is it an appliance?"

Wilbur thought for a moment but couldn't come up with a reasonable way to view it as one.

"No," he admitted.

"Then there's nothing to worry about. If it's attached you leave it. If it's not, you take it. End of story."

"Can I leave it anyway?"

Sheila adopted a reproachful expression. "Broom clean is the standard. If I work with you, I'll expect you to leave the house in good condition. Otherwise, it reflects poorly on me."

Wilbur sighed. "Fair enough. But I think you should see it anyway."

"Sorry," Sheila replied. "Musty basements disagree with me."

It struck Wilbur as odd to pursue a profession she was allergic to. Maybe she discovered this too late? Before he could press her on this or the price, Sheila smiled and darted for the door.

"Let me know when you're ready to sell," she called out before driving off.

—❖—

Of all the calls Wilbur had made or attempted to make or considered making since the fiasco began, this was the most difficult. The others were to faceless names or nameless faces, unknown and unknowable. They were guided by ephemeral hopes and fears, and entailed distant, nebulous risks.

This was different. The fear was not ephemeral, the risk neither distant nor nebulous. Wilbur was on the verge of losing something important, perhaps the only thing he truly possessed, if such a thing could be possessed at all. The call felt dangerous, final. There was the real possibility his life would be changed. Permanently, irrevocably. Not tomorrow, not in some unspecified future. Now.

Sarah always had returned before, but before there never was an ultimatum. An ultimatum he had failed to meet.

His mind drifted to little, specific things. How did she get to her sister's place? He'd never considered this before. She didn't have a car and didn't take his. Was there a bus? Maybe someone drove her. But who? Yet another thing he should know. Wilbur felt overwhelmed. There were so many things he should know. Was life really big enough to know them?

He eyed the phone. It seemed so harmless, so tranquil. Who would have guessed his fate could rest with something so small. Wilbur had no name for the presentiment he felt, nor did he care to give it one. All he could do was hope for the best. Every passing moment worsened his prospects in so many ways. The call had to be made, but haste could be catastrophic. There was some sequence of words which would bring her back, calm the waters, restore what was. Others would lead to shipwreck and a life adrift. But what were the magic words?

He had dwelt on this since she left but found himself no closer to an answer. Wilbur played and replayed in his head the myriad paths their conversation could take. How he would respond to this or that eventuality. What she could or would or may say, what it meant, and how he must reply. But this brought no measure of clarity.

He decided. He was unprepared, naked before her wrath, and utterly ill-equipped to dispel it. But he had to make the call. He would do his best and spend the remainder of his life lamenting that it had not been enough.

A bead of sweat made its way down Wilbur's forehead and clung to his brow. He almost could see the little droplet, imagine its life, envy the lucidity of its preordained path. There was no room for responsibility or regret. Did it too hope for something more? What ambition did such a thing harbor, incomprehensible to him yet no less bitter for its impotence? Perhaps the droplet would be content spilling into his eye, obscuring his vision for a moment. Wilbur wished his own path were so clear, his own hope so distinct.

Drawing a taut breath, he dialed.

A man picked up, and Wilbur's heart froze. He asked for Sarah, and the man hung up. Had she found a new life already? It hurt that nobody had told him. Glancing at his sister-in-law's number, he realized he had exchanged the last two digits. Was eliciting this mistake the droplet's entire purpose? He felt guilty foiling it.

Steadying his hand, Wilbur tried again. This time Sarah picked up. He lingered on the familiar nasality of her voice. It sounded like home.

~•~

The argument was long and serpentine. Neither fire nor water served, or perhaps Wilbur applied them in the wrong doses at the wrong times.

After nearly an hour, he found himself exhausted and sensed that Sarah was too. But they could not leave things like this. He had staked everything on this call and doubted he had the strength for another. Losing Sarah didn't seem as bad as not knowing whether he had lost her. Wilbur knew he would regret this, perhaps more than anything he ever had regretted. But he could not help the sentiment. He simply lacked the energy to fight it.

Were most of life's great decisions made through fatigue? There only had been a few, and Wilbur could not remember how they were made. Sometimes he wondered at his memory, at the impenetrable mist. Perhaps forgetting was the best way to endure. Like the pain of pregnancy, multiplied through the fault of another.

He would win her back someday, but he knew this was a fiction even as he thought it. If he could not right the ship while still afloat, what hope would there be of mending its wreckage later?

Sarah had grown quiet, and Wilbur knew the end was imminent. He had a minute, maybe less. There would be an unheralded dial-tone, then nothing. He had to do something, say something. But he could think of nothing to do or say. Everything which could be said had been.

"Please come home," he pleaded. It wasn't the first or tenth time he'd done so during the call.

The line was silent.

"Are you there?" he asked.

"I'm here." Sarah's tone was cold but carried no hostility. It sounded like she needed something from him. But what? Clearly not an apology or promise. Heaven knew there had been enough of those.

Only half-aware of what he was doing, Wilbur

began babbling about the last few days.

"It's been a real mess. Do you know I actually had a realtor over yesterday. I wish you had been here. Are they all named Sheila?"

Wilbur thought he heard sobbing but couldn't be sure. Eventually, a voice emerged from the void. It was both like and unlike his wife's.

"A realtor?"

"That's right." And with that, Wilbur sensed he had committed an irreparable blunder. Such a thing carried connotations. Why had he not realized this until now? Wilbur wished there were no connotations, no things to carry them. What else did he do which carried connotations? Maybe everything carried them. Maybe it was why the device had been delivered to him. Something he once did which carried connotations. It did not matter. He had lost her.

Wilbur wondered whether he should hang up first. It felt like the right thing to do, but he couldn't bring himself to. He would leave that to Sarah, a parting gift.

Wilbur braced himself for a dial-tone.

"I'll be home tonight," Sarah announced before hanging up.

It took a few moments for Wilbur to register her words, and even then he did not fully grasp them. What he did grasp was that she would be very unhappy about the state of the place. He got to work tidying up the week's worth of mess.

Three hours later he stood by the door, waiting for the sound of a car.

Against all hope, the next few months saw a surprising return to normality. At first Sarah was a shadow of her former self, her fire and fury gone. Wilbur was unsure whom to blame, if blame was the answer. Was it him, the protesters, the device? Was she just getting old, or was it something else altogether?

Maybe she had gone into the basement without his knowing and had been poisoned by radiation. Just because the grad student didn't find any didn't mean there wasn't any. What if he looked in the wrong places? Something had cauterized the Sarah he knew.

Over time, Sarah began to show signs of convalescence. Her replies grew sharper, her step quicker. Soon there were arguments again. Wilbur could have done without these, but his relief at having her back outweighed any unpleasantness.

In the interim, he had come to accept their plight. The device wasn't going anywhere, and their financial woes had multiplied beyond count. The penalty notices grew to fill a box, then two. However, the sheer magnitude of the burden made it easier to bear. There was no way to pay, so it was pointless to try. In the face of inescapable ruin, acceptance was the only sane choice.

A life without worry was not worth living, so Wilbur revived an old one. What if someone targeted them? If the protesters knew their address and the reporters knew their address, then everyone knew their address. Who could tell what sort of crazy attention-seeker would come after them.

But nobody did. The hate mail subsided and there were no additional protests. After one or two headlines and a particularly cruel editorial, no further mention was made of Wilbur. He had escaped the limelight. Had they decided to shun him? He hoped he'd at least get a nice obituary if someone did him in.

He probably would be remembered as that good-for-nothing who maligned the professor. What else could he be remembered for? He wished he had done something worth being remembered for. It probably was too late now. He didn't even know how to go about it. No, he would be the good-for-nothing. He could not recollect the names the protesters had called him but was certain they'd find their way into his epitaph.

Even being remembered for the device seemed preferable. Maybe that was the real reason for the delivery. The kindness of something to be remembered for. A touch of the remarkable for the unremarked. If that was the intent, it certainly misfired.

Sarah didn't speak much of their plight, and Wilbur was loathe to bring it up. What point was there? Nothing was to be done, and he would be the one doing it.

Soon after his wife's return, Wilbur was called into the director's office at work. "Attendance irregularities," the man explained. Wilbur suspected it had more to do with the publicity of the protest. Companies liked employees to be invisible and fungible. He had become uniquely visible.

Wilbur could not fault the firm. Even absent the

protest, nobody would want an employee with a nuclear bomb. Such a thing could lead to friction at work.

Though the couple's financial situation certainly wasn't helped by the loss of Wilbur's job, he found himself strangely detached about the whole thing. All he felt was guilt. Without a job, he could not provide for Sarah. He was an unnecessary husband.

Sarah's behavior was equally enigmatic. She was back to playing bridge with the professor. Wilbur learned this from Erik shortly before he was dismissed. Didn't she feel awkward doing so? She too had been affected by the whole fiasco. The professor may or may not have instigated it but certainly was the underlying cause. Sarah's willingness to overlook this seemed wildly out of character.

Or was the temperamental wife just an act? Maybe Sarah imagined it was how a wife was supposed to behave. Had she seen that in some show as a child? What if she really was a gentle soul, torn every time she pretended to be angry?

Wilbur wondered whether he too was the husband from some old television show. He tried to imagine the script and what the real Wilbur would be like. That would be a pleasant existence. Somebody else would tell him who to be and what to say and how to act. But would anybody watch a show about *him*?

Wilbur finally settled on a plausible explanation for Sarah's attitude. It likely wasn't the correct explanation or even the best explanation, but plausible would do. Sarah had to pay proper homage to the professor. That was the way back into the woman's good graces. Perhaps she missed her friend, or perhaps there were other attendant advantages. Wilbur didn't wish to pepper the idea with superfluous details. A plausible explanation required a plausible motive, nothing more. It was good enough. Though he couldn't envision Sarah paying homage to anyone, he never had seen her around other women. Maybe that was what women did: pay homage to one another.

Despite this progress, things didn't feel right to Wilbur. The problem with a return to normality was that there could be no normality. Not with that thing in the basement. And then there were the fines and penalties. The ruin these represented had been accepted in the abstract, but only in the abstract. To keep it in the abstract required action. Some payment was necessary.

Most of the threatened penalties were remote. The assessments and fines and levies would not bear down on them for months, maybe years. However dire the consequences of even a single missed deadline, the pain was not immediate. Only immediate pain demanded immediate attention. Life became a daily struggle to pay the most urgent bills. Oddly enough, Wilbur and Sarah had fewer arguments. Their conversations acquired a simple, pragmatic flavor.

As the couple's finances deteriorated, Sarah was forced to take a part-time secretarial job. Though

Wilbur initially had searched for another position, he found the waters muddied. Nobody was willing to take him. Whether this was because of the professor or the device was unclear, but it did not matter. He was reduced to sporadic mail-order work from home. They could make ends meet, as long as they ignored the mounting penalties.

Of course, things could not continue in this vein forever. Ignoring the constant stream of threats and notices was no easy task, and at some point they would have to face reality and make some difficult decisions.

By sheer coincidence, Sarah and Wilbur independently arrived at the same tactic. If a decision was deferred until too late, that decision never had to be made. Even if life still demanded a decision, there would be no urgency to it. Once it was too late, every subsequent moment would be too late as well. Why not decide in one of those moments?

This alleviated much of the stress of decision-making. It already was too late to take any meaningful action, and any action they did take would amount to nothing more than a band-aid. Wilbur wondered when the critical moment had been, the transition from possibility to impossibility. Maybe it was too late the moment the crate appeared.

The futility of action only discouraged action, not discussion. There was no harm in discussion. Discussion required no work, involved no risk, demanded no commitment. What was discussed one day could be discussed anew the next. Wilbur came to relish their discussions.

Escape was a recurring theme. When Sarah first proposed that they run away and change their names, it was half in jest — though Wilbur could not tell which half. Even when they stopped laughing and gave the idea serious consideration, it seemed outlandish. Running away and changing names were things other people did. Adventurous people who lived adventurous lives. Such things never would happen to them.

In truth, this was not the first time Wilbur had considered running away. On various occasions since the appearance of the crate, he had contemplated abandoning the house if he could not sell it. The house was the fulcrum of their misery. By abandoning it, he could abdicate responsibility for the device without imposing it on anyone. Or at least anyone specific.

This line of thought never went far, however. Wilbur had no experience hiding or fleeing and no idea where to go or what to do. He was sure he would lose what little money he had and be captured almost immediately. If anyone wanted to capture him. Part of him worried that nobody would. What could be sadder than a man who fled with nobody in pursuit.

And what if they did catch him? They probably would force him to return home. He did not think they would put him in jail. He had done nothing to merit jail. If they put him in jail, who would take the device? Who would take Sarah? They would return him to the only place he belonged, let him serve the only purpose he served. But then he'd be back to square one. All the stress and trouble and travel planning would have been for naught. The best solution was to skip that part and just remain home in the first place.

Sarah's role in those escape plans always had been unclear, nor had Wilbur ever raised the subject with her. There was no telling how she would react, and he dreaded a rebuke or worse. She likely would have thought him a coward. But there were other reasons not to tell her too. He did not wish to infect Sarah with his own despondency, and he also wasn't sure what role he wanted her to have. Sometimes, he thought of whisking her away with him. Other times, he resolved to go it alone. None of the plans had a real chance of fruition, so it was harmless to assign her whatever role he fancied.

At one point, Wilbur even imagined it would be valiant to leave Sarah behind. He would draw the world's wrath away, and she could escape or live in peace or whatever damsels did after the hero sacrificed himself. However, the apparent nobility of this did not survive scrutiny. He simply would be dumping the house, the device, and all their problems on her. She would not magically find herself free of the affair if he vanished. In fact, she would find herself alone at the center of it. Seen in this light, abandoning the house would be a singular act of cowardice.

The escape plans involving Sarah were no less implausible. Even if she agreed to join him, it wasn't clear they could make it work. They never even had taken a vacation together. There always was some reason not to. They didn't want to do the same things, or the time wasn't right, or the money wasn't there. Now, there was less money, they'd be away forever, and they would have to do the same things. They could hide from each other in a house, but not in a car or motel room. If they couldn't agree on a short trip to a definite place, how could they agree on a long trip to an indefinite one?

Wilbur eventually had stopped flirting with such ideas. Though pleasant distractions from the overwhelming stress, they lost much of their appeal once he accepted that running away was simply unrealistic.

But now escape was back on the table, with one crucial difference. Sarah had suggested it, and that made all the difference in the world. What adversity they faced, they faced together. He wouldn't have to plan by himself, terrified to tell his wife anything. She discussed things openly with him now. He wasn't alone anymore. Wilbur wondered whether Sarah felt the same way. Had she too secretly entertained such ideas this whole time, afraid to tell him for unknowable reasons of her own?

They now shared a dream, and that made Wilbur happy. However improbable the actual notion remained, it no longer was impossible. That was the magic of two. Whatever the problem, each could hope the other would discover the answer.

Their harmony of purpose infused the couple with both hope and confidence, and banished the doubts which marred Wilbur's earlier plans. He and Sarah somehow would find a way to thrive together within the constraints of a life on the run. Maybe it would be the very spur their relationship needed.

However, one concern tempered Wilbur's newfound optimism. It was a worry he could not shake. Why hadn't Sarah left him? She could run away and start life fresh, and nobody would think less of her. So why hadn't she? Wilbur was baffled by it. When she had stormed off to her sister, part of him was sure the time finally had arrived. Though at great cost to him, the world would make sense again. Was it better to be sad in a world that made sense or happy in a world that did not?

When Sarah did return, Wilbur was as confused as ever. He was very glad she had, but once again could not understand why. Even now, he still did not. Without such crucial knowledge, how could he be sure she would remain by his side or for how long? She had weathered many years of marriage to him, and there clearly was some inexplicable reason she stayed. He only could hope it endured.

The couple's new talk of escape was at first idle fancy, but it quickly moved past that. As signs of the coming storm grew, Sarah and Wilbur warmed to the idea of an adventure. An adventurous life was better than no life, even to the unadventurous. But their willingness did not address the underlying problem. If they ran, they would be pursued. Others would be suspicious. What sort of people would leave a perfectly good life behind? Why would unadventurous people run unless they had something to run from?

Hashing and rehashing this with Sarah, Wilbur realized their initial reticence could provide the answer. The two of them weren't adventurous, so why try to be? Running would not work, but there were other ways to move. They could walk or drive or take a boat. There were dirigibles and bicycles and even those skateboards that kids liked so much. He and Sarah just needed to pick an unadventurous way to move. Then they would not be running or fleeing or escaping, just moving.

There would be nothing untoward in this. People commonly reached a point in life where they desired change. When they became eccentric. Maybe he and Sarah were eccentrics, the sort of people who did such things. Nobody would wonder if eccentrics suddenly moved. Doing eccentric things was what made eccentrics eccentric.

To move without suspicion, they first needed to deal with the house. The fulcrum. Wilbur wished they could just sit back and let the bank foreclose. It would be costly relative to selling, but simple and certain. Banks wouldn't refuse to foreclose just because there was a nuclear bomb in the basement. They had policies and procedures. Unpaid mortgages had to be foreclosed upon, end of story. Nor would Wilbur feel any guilt foisting the device on a bank, especially one which had foreclosed on him.

There was one problem with this plan, however. They had no mortgage. This was the fault of Wilbur's father-in-law. When he passed away, the couple had used Sarah's inheritance to pay off the mortgage.

The only remaining option was to sell the house and start anew with the proceeds. Of course, they didn't plan to leave the place "broom-clean" and certainly didn't plan to share this fact with the realtor. She would be upset, but they could live with that. Next to the torrent of official wrath they had incurred through no fault of their own, the displeasure of a single realtor was of little consequence, even if justified. Foisting the device on an unwitting buyer troubled them more.

Wilbur and Sarah quickly convinced themselves that such compunction was misplaced. Sarah pointed out that the buyer had a choice, whereas she and Wilbur did not. The buyer would see the device when inspecting the home and realize that its removal was unrealistic. Maybe that even would be *why* they bought the place. The buyer would not be blameless.

The more the couple considered it, the more enticing the proposition grew. Every evening the plan made sense, every morning it did not. Despite the arguments in its favor, Wilbur still could not grow comfortable passing the burden to someone else. Even a stranger. Sarah never made her thoughts on this entirely clear but also seemed to have reservations despite having advocated it.

Wilbur also had another misgiving, one which was his alone. He felt he was betraying his destiny. The device had been delivered to him, not to somebody else. This was *his* profound destiny. Not Sarah's, not some stranger's. Who knew what sort of person he would be entrusting it to? Just because someone qualified for a mortgage didn't mean they qualified for a profound destiny.

What finally swayed Wilbur was something completely different, something which outweighed any of these considerations. It was the woman across the table. This was not accomplished through words or intimation or manipulation, but simply by her existence. Sarah had tied herself to him. Wilbur could allow his qualms to govern his own fate but not hers. Not that of the woman who willingly put herself in his hands. Rightly or wrongly, her future was more important than some stranger's convenience or Wilbur's destiny.

For her part, Sarah remained oddly passive when it came to the actual decision. She readily participated in the discussion but artfully refused anything more. Wilbur was unsure whether she viewed the responsibility as his or simply remained undecided. Either way, it made his deliberations more burdensome.

If she did not advocate for herself, it was incumbent on him to advocate for her. This meant scrutinizing his own motives. Conclusions which had seemed self-evident now appeared self-indulgent. Wilbur felt a mixture of guilt and tenderness toward his wife. Why didn't she speak up? It was unlike her. Maybe that was the point.

With more than a little trepidation, Wilbur called the realtor.

It turned out that all the stress and concern and deliberation was for naught. The much-anticipated call with the realtor involved three sentences, all hers. The last was "I'm sorry."

Apparently, Sheila had done some research and discovered the insurance appraisal. An uninsurable house was an unsalable house, to use her precise words. The curious result was that Wilbur felt a profound sense of relief. It was clear from Sarah's expression that she did too. They did not wish to move. Whatever their trouble at home, it was a known trouble. They had dealt with trouble at home before. Trouble at home was a matter of degree, trouble elsewhere was something new.

The next few weeks saw the skies brighten a little. The dreaded legal onslaught did not materialize. They knew it eventually would, but that did not matter. It would happen in some vague future. There was no telling how long it would take things to wend their way through the myriad unseeing bureaucracies. Each passing day felt less a reprieve, more a pardon.

Bereft of purpose, the couple's discussions soon dwindled and ceased. Sarah reverted to complete indifference, with one important change. Though she made abundantly clear that getting rid of the device remained Wilbur's responsibility, the urgency was gone. There were no ultimatums or explosions or demands, at least regarding the device. Wilbur marveled at this change. Had Sarah found meaning in her part-time job? She was no less fiery but seemed happier.

This left Wilbur and the device. Since he apparently could not get rid of the thing, there remained the question of what he *should* do with it. Erik's suggestion held no appeal. Even if Wilbur could think like an evil genius, he had no desire to. World domination sounded like lots of hard work and lots of peril. If it was easy, everyone would do it. And what would he gain by it? If getting there was a chore, Wilbur dreaded to think what staying there would entail.

Probably public speaking. He had a hard enough time with private speaking. The more he thought about it, the less attractive world domination seemed. Why go to such trouble to find misery? He already had all the misery he needed.

Maybe Andrew was right, and the device had been there all along. Why couldn't he have remained oblivious? None of this would have happened if he had remained oblivious. What if he pretended to be oblivious? Just left the device in its crate and ignored it. That wasn't quite the same as being oblivious, but maybe it would become the same. Had he done so before but forgotten?

This raised an interesting question. If he had managed not to notice the crate for so long, what else had he failed to notice? Was his life filled with the unnoticed? What if there were things he did notice which *weren't* there? He could not dismiss that possibility. If one could be true, so could the other. Was Sarah really there? Maybe she was real but married to someone else who lived right there with them. Someone Wilbur had not noticed. Was there more to her than his mind would let him see?

Wilbur's thoughts returned to the crate. It was solid, incontrovertible, and hard not to notice. Hard, but not impossible. Yes, he would do just that. He would choose not to notice it. Since he couldn't leave, this was the next best thing. The device couldn't leave either, so at least they had something in common.

Wilbur looked around. How had he ended up in the basement? He must have been lost in thought. He gave the crate an affectionate pat, then turned off the light and headed upstairs.

Sarah was in the kitchen but said nothing as he absentmindedly drifted up the stairs to the bedroom. He sat on the bed, then lay back. It was so soft. He felt he could drift off to sleep and never wake up.

How could he sleep above that thing for a moment longer, let alone forever? Knowing it was there, waiting, slowly ticking away the seconds of his life on some obscene hidden clock. Wilbur knew nothing about what it wanted, its motives. Maybe it would leak cancer into the two of them. What other than ruin and death was such a thing capable of? Sooner or later it would destroy everything he cared about. It already almost had and was bound to try again. That was its nature.

What if it really decided to? Not in some vague, metaphorical sense, but in earnest. That possibility would haunt his every breath, his every moment, his every thought. He could feel it now, forming icicles in his veins. Sarah was lucky she didn't know these things. She thought its malice was confined to attracting fines and other such trouble. She did not understand its essence, its purpose.

Wilbur wondered whether this was by design. He had assumed her refusal to discuss the device stemmed from obstinance. Perhaps it was wisdom instead, the rejection of undesirable knowledge. But how could she know what she shouldn't know? Maybe Sarah had some innate intuition.

He wished he had possessed such foresight. A wave of panic washed over Wilbur, followed by the additional panic of knowing panic. How long could he last like this? And why hadn't he felt it before? Perhaps it was the removal of hope. He and the thing weren't just housemates, they were cellmates. Until the day he died, the house would be his. Until the day he died, he would sleep above a 1.72 megaton nuclear bomb of unknown origin and unknown purpose. And *it* would decide which day that would be. Yes, he had the control button. Yes, this thing had been given to him, placed under him, assigned to him. Yes, he was its master. But how long would he have mastery over it? Or himself.

Wilbur glanced at the small lamp-table by the bed. Without rising, he slid open the drawer and fumbled around. His hand emerged with the little box. The blind groping must have popped it open, and he slowly pressed it shut. With a shudder, Wilbur realized how careless he had been. How close he had come. Not close enough.

The choice was his, for now. One day he would have no choice. It would be taken from him, along with everything else. One day or one month or one hour or one second. Who could say whether it or he would fail first. Wilbur wondered whether the device would work, whether he would be disappointed if it did not. The box popped open again.

As Wilbur's finger reached for the button, a wave of satisfaction poured over him, driving before it the chill and emptiness and fear. His hand was still and steady. Satisfaction rose into ecstasy, then resolved into quiet pride. The pride of a soldier whose courage passed muster, of a composer putting the last stroke on his last symphony. The pride of expectation fulfilled, of a job accomplished.

It would be another's burden to judge his work, a judgment of no consequence. Nobody could deprive Wilbur of the past. Of a decision *he* made. Of a deed *he* accomplished. Of a thing done by his will and his alone.

Perhaps that was why he existed: to make a single binary choice. That was the measure of his will, its heft and breadth and potency. What was a man whose will did not matter? What was a man who refused his choice when it came? There could be no greater cowardice. This would be his redemption, erasing his decades of failure to be who he should have been. What greater legacy could he hope for?

Wilbur was alive, and nothing else mattered. *That* was the power of the thing in the basement. That and blowing everybody up.

The box snapped shut, and Wilbur quietly returned it to the drawer. He rose and patted the wrinkles from his shirt.

"Hon, when is dinner?" he called out.

"Whenever I say it is," a shrill voice replied from downstairs.

Wilbur smiled.

⟭ **THE END** ⟬

Also Available

THE MAN WHO STANDS IN LINE

Killer flies, amorous dinosaurs, angry buildings, and one very large fish — all in a single volume. This quirky collection of flash fiction, vignettes, and poetry is variously absurd, dark, and comic. A monstrous blister, the secret to immortality, and a lost piece of brain are just a few other oddities one will encounter in this one-of-a-kind book.

"...the lasting impression of the writing within is without question. Don't let their brevity fool you; these works are tenacious, earnest, and overflowing with gloom."

— Kirkus Review

THE WAY AROUND

More absurd, horrifying, and downright inexplicable shorts from the mind of K.M. Halpern. Included are such soon-to-be classics as Buzz-Saw Bob, the sport of pendulum watching, yet another secret to ultimate success, the art of gasping, a neighbor who is definitely not Mr. Rogers, and Buddha's morning commute.

I legally can't promise that this book will transform you into the demiurge you were meant to be. All I can say is that no medical studies have proved otherwise and the FDA moves very slowly.

Available through Amazon, B&N, and bookstores everywhere.

Also Available

THE LAST CLOUD

Meet the superhero Spleen Squeezer, discover the true story of Eden, and travel to the safest city in the world in this 3rd collection of unclassifiable ultra-short pieces. But wait, there's MORE!!!! For the same price, you get twice the wisdom, twice the wit, twice the heartpounding absurdity. Learn the danger of having ears, the importance of being unlikable, and how to achieve quality as an executioner. But it's a limited time offer. Delay and it could be too late. Don't condemn yourself to an eternity of unrelenting regret. Buy now, Now, NOW. Operators are standing by. Don't you realize how inconsiderate it is to keep them waiting?

PACE

In this dark new sci-fi thriller by MIT PhD K.M. Halpern, a mysterious "Front" appears in Scotland and slowly expands outward, threatening humanity's existence. In defiance of the known laws of physics, it only kills humans and is otherwise undetectable. As panic-stricken nations struggle against both the advancing menace and a tide of civil unrest, desperate individuals must find their own paths and find them quickly. The slow-moving Front may seem easy to escape, but in this near-future few things are as they seem.

A pitch-black global thriller that is nevertheless supremely intimate. — *Kirkus Review*

Available through Amazon, B&N, and bookstores everywhere.

Audiobooks

The Man Who Stands in Line

The Way Around

The Last Cloud

Available through Audible, iTunes, and Amazon.

ACKNOWLEDGMENTS

First, I would like to thank Alex C. The general idea for this novella was inspired by one of our many interesting conversations.

I also would like to thank Meia G, Alvin H, Patrick O, and Naturi T for many valuable thoughts and suggestions on my initial draft. Meia G also deserves a second thanks for kindly proofreading the final manuscript.

My thanks to C.M. Adams for her insightful comments as a professional editor and to Sara Zieve Miller for her wonderful drawings.

Finally, I would like to thank whoever delivered a gigantic, immovable crate to my basement, as well as whatever global conspiracy, shadow government, sinister corporation, alien empire, or typo is behind it. Feel free to come collect it at your earliest convenience.

ABOUT THE AUTHOR

K.M. Halpern was born in New York and, after spending far too much time there, finally returned to the Cambridge, MA he knew and loved from graduate school. Unfortunately, the entire city had transformed into an impenetrable tangle of bicycles of all shapes and sizes.

Some had only a single wheel, others as many as seventeen and a half. On a few, the number changed in time to some silent rhythm. The cyclists rode on sidewalks and lawns, through living rooms and telephone wires, and even into several of the compactified dimensions of string theory.

Despite the reckless speeding, frequent collisions, and constant barking of complaints and warnings, the cyclists never actually got anywhere. There remained only a single functioning bike rental station, and all rides started and ended there. Nobody could object to this, because it was only natural that cyclists would move in a cycle.

The constant danger and obstruction and aggression seemed pointless, but K.M. was assured by the parties involved that it was environmentally friendly danger and obstruction and aggression — and therefore preferable to the alternatives.

Unable to safely venture outside, K.M. presently spends his time in front of a small rectangular device typing symbols that those who appreciate do not understand and those who understand do not appreciate.

K.M. holds a PhD in theoretical physics from MIT, more commonly known as 'that place in the movies that used to do science before being purchased by venture capital.' He may be found at https://www.kmhalpern.com and providing sports commentary from his deck on the lethal maelstrom below.

www.ingramcontent.com/pod-product-compliance
Lightning Source LLC
Chambersburg PA
CBHW030628190726
48286CB00008B/2437